SUMMER AT BLUE SANDS COVE

CP WARD

For Cracky
This is not supposed to be about you

SUMMER AT BLUE SANDS COVE

1

WEEKDAY BLUES

'I'M COMING!'

The man in the business suit had his hand in the air, waving it back and forth as though directing a plane to land. Carrying the tray in one hand, Grace Clelland weaved her way through the packed tables as the customer's expression slowly changed from a peculiar look of frustration to one of outright anger.

She had only just lowered the tray to the table and begun to offload the drinks when he shook his head.

'No, no, no. I ordered soy latte. This is whole milk.'

Grace looked at the glass of brown liquid topped with whipped cream and strawberry sauce, a little flag with the café's logo poking triumphantly out of the top.

'It says soy latte on the receipt,' Grace said, nodding at the piece of paper poking out from underneath.

'Are you calling me a liar?'

Grace gave a vehement shake of the head. 'No, of course not. It's just that the receipt says—'

The man poked a finger at the glass, tapping it with a manicured fingernail. 'You can tell from the way the liquid swirls that it's whole milk. Do you people think I'm stupid? What, do you save a quid or something? You think once I start to drink I won't bother to complain?'

Grace had no words. She shook her head openmouthed, glancing up at the suit's companions, two similarly attired men, their shirts alone worth more than a month of Grace's salary, their hair ruffled in a magazine-styled way, stubble just apparent enough to suggest they liked to go canoeing or wilderness hiking in their free time when not running up millions on stock deals. Both pouted. One winked and turned up a corner of his mouth in a gesture which was equal parts come on and disgust. On top of the latte, the little flag began to tilt in a gesture of surrender.

'What's that accent anyway?' the first man said, frowning again. 'Romanian? A bit of a problem now they're shutting the borders, isn't it?'

Grace winced. 'Cornwall.'

The man shrugged. 'Same difference. All gypsies, aren't you?'

Grace held her breath, resisting the urge to pitch the drink over the man's expensive shirt. While her manager Don might approve, he would have to fire her in order to save money for the lawsuit.

'I'll get you a replacement, *sir*,' Grace said, refusing to meet his eyes as she scooped the tray up and spun on her heels before she could think to do anything else. From behind her she heard a snigger.

'Look, she's got straw poking out of her skirt.'

'O-da-lay-ha-ho.'

Snorts of laughter. Someone thumped the table top, and chair legs creaked as another man rocked back and forth.

Grace closed her eyes and gritted her teeth. A moment

later the kitchen doors swung open and she entered the safety of the staff area.

'The toff on table nine says we've used whole milk instead of soy,' she said to no one in particular, quickly setting the tray down on the stainless steel unit before she gave in to her frustration and threw it down instead. 'And he called me a gypsy. I'm going on a break.'

She headed for a back door that led out of the kitchen and into a short corridor which opened outside. She pulled off her apron and hat and pushed out through the doors into the Bristol sunshine. Two older waitresses were already outside, both smoking. Grace gave one a shrug, muttering, 'Bankers lunchtime is the worst.'

'Just one letter you need to replace and you're there, dearie,' said one of the other waitresses. 'Never done a day of real work in their lives. It's why they use computers. Their hands are so soft they get tissue cuts.'

Grace smiled, then took out her phone and walked a few paces up the alley, wanting to be alone. She pulled up her ongoing conversation with Joan and typed a quick message.

Weekday lunchtime blues … I've been hit on three times—two guys and one girl—asked the best place for a discount hair stylist, and told there's a sale on in TK Maxx so I can upgrade my footwear. And I got called a gypsy.

There's a sale on in TK Maxx?? There's a train that leaves here in ten minutes. Call in sick tomorrow and we're there.

Grace smiled, then typed her reply. *All quiet down there?*

Surf's flat so we've got all the hunks in the café eating pasties. Air's so full of testosterone I'm growing pecs just from breathing it in.

I need pictorial evidence.

Of my pecs?

Of the guys!

Joan was typing. Grace waited patiently for a reply, but

the next message that flashed up wasn't from Joan but from Gavin. She felt a little tingle in her stomach as she opened it, but it wasn't what she was expecting.

We need to talk. Can you come over tonight?

Grace stared. They'd been dating just two months. It was the first message that she'd ever received without an *xx*. Something was up.

Seriously, it's raining so the place is dead, but Blue Sands looks all right in the rain anyway, and there's a ton of books on the stand that I haven't read. I wish you'd come down and visit. I miss you so much.

What's up?

It's raining, I just told you. Forecast said sun so we ordered a ton of pasties in. Silver linings—who gets to eat them??

Grace frowned. *Sorry, that was meant for Gavin. He just messaged me. He must have seen I was online.*

Gavin? That's the new guy? The guy with the Range Rover?

It's a Rover Mini. But it's only two years old. Yeah. The guy I met in the gym.

Smooooooooth….

Grace blushed. She glanced up at the other waitresses on break outside the doors, but one was smoking another cigarette and the other was having a loud conversation on her phone with a car rental firm.

It really wasn't. I nearly spilled a coffee on him by the vending machine. Hang on, I just have to message him.

Is everything all right?

I'll tell you later.

Grace felt a sinking feeling in the pit of her stomach. She was about to message Gavin again when the door opened behind her.

'Clelland! This isn't a working holiday!'

Grace raised a hand at Don, the manager, leaning around the back door. 'I'm coming!' she called.

I've got to go, she typed to Joan. And to Gavin, she said, *I'll call you later.*

As she jogged for the back door, mentally steeling herself for another round of abuse from overpaid button pushers, her phone beeped once.

Love you, Joan's message said. *Please come and visit. It's been too long.*

2

TEMPTATIONS

It didn't bode well that Gavin suggested a neutral location for their evening meeting, a park which happened to be a couple of miles closer to his place than to hers. She got off the bus, walked up the street and through the park gate, only to be confronted with Gavin standing by a fountain in his running gear, already warming up.

'Hi,' Grace said, approaching him. 'Should I have come prepared? I dressed for something a little more casual.'

Gavin shook his head. 'You look fine.'

Fine. Just *fine.* It was what her mother would have said before a job interview.

He was all thick shoulders, lycra running trousers, and an expensive Mont Bell running jacket, his breath puffing out in little gasps as he pumped his legs up and down.

'Did you want me to hold your stopwatch or something?' Grace asked, the sinking feeling that had left her unable to eat anything after lunch making way for something just a little more hopeful, that her sports-mad new boyfriend wanted something other than what she had been suspecting all day. Perhaps he was planning to run around the world or something. Only five people had supposedly done it, and while it might mean they were apart for most of the next two years, at least it was something she could—in a superficial way, at least —support.

'I wanted to talk. About us.'

Nope. It was heading in the same direction that her other relationships had gone.

'Look, just get it over with. I like you, Gavin, but it's only been a couple of months. I can handle it. You don't think we fit well enough. That's okay.'

It wouldn't matter that it was the fourth guy in three years who would duck out before the three-month mark had passed. Grace would get over it; she would drink and message-Joan her way through it, like she had the previous three. The world wouldn't end, even if it felt like it might for a while.

Gavin gave her a pained smile. 'You're kind, Grace,' he said. 'And there's a lot to like about you. I mean it. It's just … there are a couple of things.'

Which I don't need to hear.

'Like what?'

Gavin grimaced again and Grace hoped he would save her the humiliation of a list. But when he cleared his throat, she knew it was coming. Perhaps that was why he had worn his running gear: so he could get away.

'You get up too late,' he said. 'I mean, you're not going to get anywhere in life getting up at seven, are you? The day's half done. And you have no ambition. You're what, thirty-five and you work in a café.'

'I'm twenty-eight.'

Gavin sighed. 'Well, you look thirty-five. Okay, maybe

that's harsh. Thirty-two at least. It must be the way you do your hair. I mean, can't you go somewhere a little more upmarket?'

Instead of ripping off one of her shoes and hitting him around the head with it, Grace just felt an easy sense of resignation. Best to let him have his moment and be done with it.

'I have a mortgage to pay,' she said. 'I don't live with my parents, Gavin.'

He scowled. 'That was cheap. It's temporary.'

'You're calling me cheap?'

He obviously misunderstood. 'Look, I appreciate that you always contribute to dinner when we go out, picking up the odd.'

'I always pay half! It's you who "picks up the odd".'

Gavin ignored her. 'It's very modern of you. But your money doesn't impress me.'

Grace sighed. 'You'd have low standards if it did.'

'I'm just not a materialistic guy.'

Grace could have picked five labels off his current attire which suggested otherwise, but she was too tired to prolong this torture any longer than necessary.

'Goodbye, Gavin. It was nice, for a while.'

She started to turn away, but he danced around her like some kind of exercise fairy, doing little sidesteps, puffing out his breath in short, sharp gasps.

'But the worst is the snoring,' he said. 'Honestly, you should have someone check that. It gave me night terrors. I thought I'd got over my childhood traumas, but since I met you, the nightmares I've had … they've been strong. I'll say that. Strong.'

'I'm sorry that your childhood sucked.'

Gavin shook his head. 'I opened the car door and fell out on my parents' drive when I was just five years old,' he said. 'A lorry was passing on the other side of the street, and the sound left me crying for a week. So my mother said. And your snoring brought that sound back. I'm going to a therapist tomorrow. I don't like to say this, but I think you could have ruined my life.'

Grace smiled. 'Nothing that a bit of exercise won't fix.'

'Are you trying to be funny? Is that all you thought of our relationship? Like it was a big joke? Or did you just get together with me out of some sadistic need to make a person suffer?'

'I—'

'If that's your attitude, then I think I'm better off without you.'

Grace just stared. Gavin's cheeks puffed out like a frog about to croak. She wondered if he was hyperventilating.

'Do you want me to pat you on the back? Will it help?'

Gavin shook his head. 'Words fail me,' he said. 'Was this a set up from the start?'

Quite unsure how being dumped had twisted around to her ruining Gavin's life, Grace shrugged. 'I think I'll be going home now,' she said.

Before Gavin could respond, she started walking away.

'I've changed spinning classes!' he shouted. 'If I see you again I'll have flashbacks!'

Grace sighed, pulled her bag up over her shoulder, and ran to catch a bus which was just pulling into the bus stop outside the park gates.

It didn't matter where it was going.

⁓

Chipping Sodbury, so it turned out.

Grace bought a kebab in a Turkish takeaway across the street from the little bus station, and sat on the one chair by the window to eat while she waited for a return bus, her phone beside her.

Prickprickprickprick, was Joan's first message. *You just dodged a bullet.*

Another one, Grace answered.

We've got a lovely sunset tonight. You should visit. Can't you jack in your job? I can find hours for you at the café.

Grace paused before replying. Her teens had been good years, working alongside Joan in the Blue Sands Café, owned by Joan's parents, but she was twenty-eight now and didn't need a backwards step. Plus, it would only be for the summer. At least her job now—bankers, be damned—was year-round, even if a future in the catering industry was hardly turning out like she had hoped.

Her phone buzzed again; Joan had sent a picture. Grace opened it up and smiled: a miserable scene of rain teeming down the window with the vague outline of a sandy cove in the background.

You lied.

Just like the tourist brochures. Doesn't it make you feel at home? Remember all those summers we spent drinking cider in the chalets because it rained so hard even the sea got annoyed? Come on, Graceful. Give me one more. It's so boring here without you.

A throwback summer. It was very tempting.

I'll think about it, she messaged back.

Come on. And with all those spinning classes, you can finally take on the Hill of Suffering. You could be the first official local to cycle faster than walking pace. Come on, Graceful. You know you want to.

I'll think about it, Grace messaged again, then closed her messaging app before Joan had enough time to convince her.

And anyway, the bus was coming. If she was lucky, she'd still be back in time for spinning class. Gavin be damned. He was nothing on Mike Anderson anyway.

3

SPINNING

Although it kept her fit like nothing ever had in her life before, Grace would be the first to admit—drunkenly, to Joan, at least—that she had signed up for spinning classes in order to get in the kind of shape that would one day allow her to cycle all the way from the bottom to the top of Melrose Hill—what local kids had called the Hill of Suffering for as long as she could remember—both without stopping and at faster than walking pace. No official local had ever done it. Some smarmy bastard called Matt who had done a few stages of the Tour de France had visited one summer and pulled it off, but he had moved away shortly after and therefore didn't officially count.

Grace, captain of her university road racing team, had always dreamed of returning home one summer, years after disappearing out into the world, to wow everyone from school who still lived in the area with her cycling prowess, and prove once and for all that she wasn't the lush they all remembered.

Not all of the time, at any rate.

Over the years her road racing prowess had faded into weekend leisure rides, but you had to go a long way in South Gloucestershire to find any decent hills. Spinning class had proven the antidote to her flat-road bullying, and the thought of taking down the Hill of Suffering had been her motivation.

And then she had met her instructor.

The spinning class was so popular you had to show up thirty minutes early to be sure of getting a bike, and Mike Anderson, he of the back muscles and buns to die for, had proven why. A minor celebrity—after a brief career in a failed nineties' boy-band he had done the naughties' rounds of the reality TV shows before starting a career as a fitness instructor—he had matured into a forty-something dreamboat which had all of the women and some of the men drooling over his physique, his smile, and his take-me-home-for-tea eyes.

Grace joined the queue to enter, Mike standing by the door as always, greeting each attendee like an old friend. When her time came, she couldn't bring herself to speak, only to stare into his dreamy eyes and make a throaty grunt.

'Grace … how lovely to see you. You look well, but … you're troubled by something, aren't you? Hit that bike hard tonight, my love. It'll clear out whatever negativity has been building up.'

And she was past, without even responding, but with a delightful warmth in her heart as behind her, Mike asked about another customer's cat.

'Neutering can be traumatic, can't it? But Bobby will be fine in a couple of days, you'll see.'

With Mike's seeming clairvoyance driving her on, Grace was ready to hit new heights tonight, to exorcise her memory of Gavin once and for all. As Mike straddled his bike at the front of the group, on a machine that rather bizarrely stood on a revolving pedestal in order that over the course of the class all the attendees could get a full view of every angle of their godlike instructor, Grace readied herself to hit higher speeds and greater elevations than ever before. Hill of Suffering indeed. It would look like a children's slide the next time she went home.

'Oh, that's not good.'

Mike, speaking into a microphone in his smooth, milky voice, sounded a little alarmed. Most of the people who had been warming up with a few brisk revolutions came to a stop and watched their instructor, barely daring to breathe.

Mike climbed back off the bike and began to stretch his right leg.

'Well, excuse me for a moment. It appears I might have tweaked my groin. If you could wait a moment, ladies and guys, I'll go put a little spray on it and see if we can't get through the class that way.'

And he was gone, out through the studio doors, leaving the attendees to mutter to each other in hushed, fearful voices. What had happened? Would Mike be able to continue the class? And if he was injured, how long would he be unable to ride?

He returned a few minutes later, visibly limping. He climbed up on to the pedestal and stood shaking his head. His cheeks even appeared damp as though he'd been crying.

'I'm sorry to inform you all of this, but I'm afraid it's quite a serious tweak. I won't be able to ride for at least a month.'

'Will the class be cancelled?' someone near the front wailed, as other attendees began to sniff, one or two to cry. 'I can't get by without this. I need you, Mike.'

'And I need you guys too. You're my flock. But this is just one of those things that happens sometimes. In a month or two I'll be fine, and I'll be back on the bike again, and it'll be like I was never away. However, I can't leave you without an instructor, so I've found someone to cover for me.' He lifted a hand and indicated the door, just as it swung open.

A woman in a vest and combat trousers stood there, her muscled arms mottled with tattoos. Frizzy black hair was tied back and she wore a sour pout as she looked around the room. A vicious scar had punctured her cheek, leaving behind a red star shape which appeared to have been coloured in with felt tip pen.

The woman stalked through the group to the front, fists clenched as though spoiling for a fight. Mike smiled and waved her to stand next to him.

'This is Doreen,' he said. 'She'll be taking over as your instructor until my groin is back in tip top shape.' Then, unclipping the microphone and headset, he handed it across.

'Over to you,' came his last soft words, and then he was walking out of the room, giving regretful waves as he passed, comforting a couple of people who were crying, reassuring the same woman as before that her cat would be fine.

The door closed behind him, and the room felt suddenly cold.

'All right, you scum, on your bikes,' Doreen snapped, climbing up onto the instructor's bike. 'I just got out of prison. You want to know how you survive in prison? You train, and you fight. Are you ready to train and fight, you worms?'

A couple of people shouted 'Yeah!', but most people just looked afraid.

'Faster, scum!' Doreen shouted. 'You're in the prison yard, and some gang boys have got a beef. They're coming after you. You're not man enough to take them down, so what are you going to do? Train, train, train!'

The whir of the spinning bikes wasn't quite loud enough to cover the gasps from the desperate riders.

'You know how I got this scar? Some punk in the mess hall fleeced me half an egg. You know how much damage a plastic spoon can do? I took a tray in the face for my troubles but he's walking with a limp for the rest of his life. Faster, worms!'

Grace, unsure how a plastic spoon could cause a limp but not willing to ask, gritted her teeth and pedaled. She felt like she'd climbed the Hill of Suffering a dozen times over. She glanced at the clock. Five minutes left. A handful of people had already run out of the room in tears, and those who remained looked ready to break.

'What do you get if you cross a crowbar with a broken axe handle?' Doreen asked, pedaling at a manic speed with seemingly no trouble. 'A whole world of hurt. Are you feeling the pain yet, you useless rats? No pain, all the shame. If you're not broken you can't be fixed, and from the look of you soft-bellied turkeys there's a lot of fixing that needs to be done. Train, train, train!'

And then it was over. Doreen jumped off her bike and stalked among the remaining riders, arms glistening with sweat.

'Did you do your best?' she asked, looking around as though searching for guilty faces. 'If you didn't, if you slacked off for one second, now's your chance to confess.'

Most people looked too exhausted to speak, but a couple slunk out from the back and stood in front of

Doreen with their heads lowered. Grace didn't know their names but she recognised their type: they were the hardcore who went to all the classes they could, and no amount of training was ever enough.

'I confess,' said the man.

'I confess too,' said the woman.

'You worthless scum,' Doreen said, shaking her head. 'Get down and give me fifty. Now!'

The two got on the floor and started doing press-ups. At about twenty-five, Doreen put one foot on the backs of each and had them lift her. As she rose up and down like some nightmarish jack-in-the-box, arms folded and a scowl on her face, she looked around the rest of the group.

'These two are brave,' she said, even as the woman began to cry. 'They have guts, spirit, heart. The rest of you are weak, spineless worms. I know you didn't try hard enough, but you were too scared to confess. Fear is your greatest enemy. Fear loses fights. Fear breaks you. Do not be afraid. Over the next few classes I will beat the fear out of you. Class dismissed.'

As the two confessors finished their press-ups and collapsed in a heap, the others hurried to get out of the room before Doreen singled them out for any further punishment. Grace grabbed her bag and ran for the changing rooms. By the time she got there, a couple of girls were being sick, others were crying. Grace patted the arm of one, who was fumbling with a pack of cigarettes.

'Jenny, you mustn't smoke in here.'

Jenny's arm shook. 'Do you want one?'

Grace gave her a reassuring smile. 'Tempting as it is, I'll pass.'

'Anyone got any booze?' someone asked.

'I do,' someone else answered, voice unsteady.

'Someone go and ask if they've got any paper cups on reception.'

With a regretful smile around the changing room which had once been filled with laughter and casual chat at the end of every class, Grace shouldered her bag and headed out, not even wanting to stay long enough to shower. If Doreen was their new instructor, it was time to look for a different gym, or perhaps give up spinning entirely.

As she headed outside, the cool evening air shocking her still-sweaty body, her phone buzzed in her pocket.

How was spinning class?

Grace smiled. *It sucked. Magic Mike has hurt his groin. His replacement is this ex-con nutjob. I think I'm going to quit. I don't think I could survive another class.*

One more reason to come down and stay for the summer. This morning I got a text from Ben. The school kid we hired last summer? He's going surfing in South Africa this year so I need someone to work his hours at the café.

Grace stared at her phone for a long time. How would it be, going back? She hadn't lived in Blue Sands for a decade, and time had fuzzed out all the stuff she didn't like —the terrible weather, the idiot tourists, the greater idiot locals who'd gone nowhere in their lives—leaving only the good stuff.

The evenings on the beach. The barbeques. The rollers offshore, and the shirtless guys sitting on the promenade. The sunsets, the clink of pint glasses, the call of seabirds and the salty aroma of the sea.

She had been a teenager when she left. Now she was a grown woman with a job and a flat. Responsibilities.

She couldn't go back, but the temptation was there, she had to admit.

I'll think about it.

4

BREAKING POINT

'You don't snore, love,' Lisa Clelland said, absently stirring her coffee with an easy smile on her face. 'Well, not that much. Your father and I would just shut the door if you were trumpeting too loud.'

'Trumpeting?'

'Oh, I'm only having a joke. It's because you sleep on your back. If you sleep on your side you won't snore.'

'Is that medically proven?'

'That's how I fixed your father. Whenever he started to roar I just pushed a couple of pillows against his back and rolled him over. It's a genetic thing. All depends on the shape of your little dangly bit.'

'My what?'

'Your uvula. That thing in the back of your throat.'

'Is that what it's called? I literally never wondered.'

'That's it. Can't do anything about it, unless you have it cut out, and no one wants to do that, do they? Exercise and healthy living help. You don't drink or smoke anymore, do you?'

'I've never smoked and I don't have any friends to drink with.'

'Well, that's a blessing, perhaps.' Lisa stood up. 'You don't have any friends? What have you been doing these last few years?'

'Mostly working to pay my extortionate mortgage.'

'Well, if you will insist on living in the city. Life's much cheaper out in the countryside. More relaxing, too.'

'I live in Downend. It's about as far out of the city as it's possible to be without actually being out of the city. I'm a stone's throw from the ring road.'

Lisa chuckled. 'Still inside the city walls, then. Just make sure you get as much fresh air as you can. Anyway, I'd better get back to work, love. Have a good afternoon.'

As Grace watched her mother walk out of the café and head downhill towards the bank where Lisa worked, she took a deep breath and looked at her watch. Her shift started in twenty minutes. It was Friday. Friday afternoons were the worst.

With a regretful glance through the window at the boutique shops that lined Park Street down towards the Waterfront, she picked up her bag and headed out.

Three years she had worked in Jones's, the big, open plan café-bar at the top of Park Street, overpriced to meet its overpaid and under-mannered clientele. Wealth did funny things to people, making them obnoxious and entitled, condescending to those who scurried at their proverbial feet, providing the services which greased their jet-setting lifestyle. And booze on top of wealth could make people unbearable.

By personal choice, Grace only worked daytime shifts,

but Friday afternoon was when many of the customers enjoyed a lunchtime tipple.

It was packed as usual when she arrived. Feeling more reluctant than she had in months, she was already in a bad mood before she began her shift, but within a few minutes of whistles, snapped fingers, and phone-number requests, she was like a volcano with a top about to blow. As she carried a tray of complicated coffee-based drinks out through the kitchen doors, she caught the eye of her manager, Don.

Be good, his eyes said.

She was halfway across the floor when someone tugged on her skirt. A group of suits sat around a table, menus in hand.

'Hey lassie,' said the nearest man, an older, balding guy. 'Sex cossies, please. Straight.'

'Excuse me?'

'Lassie, sex cossies, please, when you have a minute.'

Grace felt her cheeks burning. The man's face looked innocent enough, but those of his companions wore pained expressions, as though his attempt at a joke had been perceived as a bad idea but no one dared to say.

'Lassie?'

A switch flipped. 'I'm not a dog, and I'm not some costume-wearing prostitute,' she snapped.

And before she could stop herself, the tray turned in her hand. Four large coffees cascaded down over the man, lumps of marshmallow and chocolate rolling down his suit like the debris of a landslide.

From behind her came a sharp cry. 'Grace Clelland! In the office … *now.*'

~

I got suspended for a month without pay.

Ouch.

Turned out the guy had just had vocal cord surgery and they were celebrating his return to work.

Double ouch. What are you going to do?

Not sure.

Hang on a minute.

The phone buzzed with an incoming call. Grace clicked receive and a moment later Joan's jovial face filled the screen.

'Hello lovely, my fingers are getting tired. Tell Auntie Joany about everything.'

'Did you dye your hair?'

Joan's chubby fingers flicked orange strands against her phone's camera. 'Do you like it? Sand orange. But let's not talk about me. Things don't sound good.'

'My life is coming to an end. I've got enough savings for a couple of months, but that's about it.'

'What are you drinking?'

Grace held up the glass. 'Australian Merlot. Two for one in Tesco.'

'Planning for the future, that's a good sign. You're not giving up just yet.'

'Not until the day after tomorrow at least.'

'Come on, you know you have a get-out clause. Without Ben I really need someone in the café, and if you won't help then I'll have to hire some other school kid. Usually I get a bunch coming in at this time of year asking around but these days they're all YouTubers and Instagrammers. No one wants to spend a summer serving ice-cream unless I pay them double minimum wage. Come on, Graceful, you know you want to.'

'Half of me does, but you know how it is. I'm supposed to be making something of my life. I can't go back to sitting on the beach every night and drinking in the Low Anchor. Those were good days, but those were teenage days. I'm twenty-eight now. It's different for you because you actually own the café. It's your business. For me it would just be a summer job.'

Joan gave a slow nod. 'Technically it's Mum's café, but we'll let that slide.'

'You know what I mean.'

'What I think you mean is that there'll be more talent in the jobseekers queue in Downend than in the ice-cream queue at Blue Sands Cove?'

'Hardly likely. But I'm not into picking up a sixteen-year-old kid.'

'Grab a granny nights were always fun. Remember how we laughed when Tim Pascoe tried to pull your mum?'

'Oh my, he had no idea.'

'Good days, Graceful. And times have changed. We don't get the kids here anymore, not now it's so cheap to go out to Spain or France or wherever. It's all families, old people, and couples. Quite sedate really. And it still rains all the bloody time, so me and you can sit around and read the books on the rack, drink coffee and talk about the old days.'

'Sounds nice.'

'I miss you, Graceful. You're my best friend. I tried filling that void with a few of the locals, but no one fits. No one's nearly as fun as you. I was that desperate I even went to the cinema with Becky Rendle once, and you can imagine how that went.'

'She talked the whole way through it?'

'Talked? She shouted. You'll never guess who she's married to now. Anyway, come on, Graceful. I miss you.'

'I miss you too.'

'Come on.'

Grace took a swig of her wine and topped up the glass from the bottle. To her dismay, she only had a little left at the bottom.

'I'll think about it,' she said, already thinking about it *a lot*.

5

ESCAPE

'You think you're fit, you scum?' Doreen said from the instructor's bike. 'You think you're fit? Twenty minutes, that's all. That's how long any of you would last in the exercise yard. When a gang comes and asks you to press eighty and you max out at twenty-five, what do you think happens? You clean a lot of toilets, that's what. With your hair. Are you hearing me? Now train. Train, train, train.'

The end of the session couldn't come soon enough. Just fifteen people had shown up tonight, with more than half the bikes empty. Not that Doreen seemed to care as she called out people to confess. Grace, keeping her head down, managed to escape into the changing rooms, where she sat in silence for a while, a towel covering her face.

A policeman had shown up at her house that afternoon to take a statement. The man she had poured coffee over had accused her of aggravated assault.

Grace hadn't bothered to defend herself. In tears, she had explained to the police officer—who had actually been rather sympathetic—that she'd reached a point where she flipped. He suggested that while she waited to find out whether she would be charged, she take a rest and do some exercise. And drink plenty of water.

Out in the lobby, she bought the most caffeinated drink she could find. As she sat drinking it at a table, a young man in a tracksuit approached.

'Excuse me, are you Grace Clelland?'

'Yes?'

'I'm John Barnwell. Gavin Barnwell's brother?'

'Oh, right.'

John Barnwell sighed and shook his head. 'I just wanted to let you know that thanks to you, Gavin is in a bad way. He told me what you do to him, the nightly torment. He's quit his job, and it looks like he'll be moving into an assisted living facility to help him through his night terrors.'

'Is this a joke?'

A tear dribbled down John Barnwell's cheek. 'Do I look like I'm joking? You've destroyed my brother's life. Are you proud of yourself? What kind of person are you, to victimize someone so fragile? You should be ashamed.'

To Grace's dismay, she realised John Barnwell was shouting. As a manager appeared, glared at Grace, then took John's arm and led him away to a staff office, Grace caught Doreen watching her from the door to the spinning studio.

'Ruining lives, are you, Clelland?' she growled. 'That's called karma. I saw you slacking off in there. Couldn't ride a tricycle, you. *Karma.*'

As Doreen went back into the studio, Grace stared at the drink in her hand, wishing it was three-quarters vodka, or something stronger.

'Well, it's not the most desirable area, but I do have a couple of people looking,' the letting agent said. 'Summer rental only?'

Grace nodded. 'For now, but we'll see what happens.'

'Well, I don't think I can get the rates you were asking for, not at such short notice.' She slid a sheet of paper across the table. 'I have each client estimate what they'd be willing to pay. Here's what I have right now.'

Grace looked at the figures and sighed. 'I'll barely cover the mortgage.'

'If you were willing to wait six months or offer a longer leasing period….'

Grace remembered the fabled Summer of Rain, 2009, when it had chucked it down throughout the entire month of August, with temperatures peaking at fifteen Celsius. Grace had been sixteen, and the summer a total washout. She and Joan and a few others had set up an awning at the top of the beach and sat under it to eat pasties and ice-cream, and have barbeques in the evening, even as the rain pelted down so hard that even at high tide they could barely see the shoreline.

It had been the worst of summers but the best of times.

'I'll take whatever you've got,' she said.

Coming out of the letting agent, she felt like a weight had lifted off her shoulders.

I'm coming, she messaged Joan from the steps outside. *Hold a job for me.*

Graceful!!!! I can't wait. Just like old times.

Grace frowned. *I just have to check with the police that it's okay.*

The assault charge? Don't worry. Just say you slipped.

I already said it was intentional.
Claim insanity. Fingers crossed they might let you off.
Fingers crossed. And toes.

A disinterested police officer jotted down her intended new address and told her to have a good time. In the crime-filled wasteland of inner-city Bristol, she suspected that a tray of coffees thrown in anger was low priority. Not that it made her feel any better, but at least she was free to leave.

It took a couple of days to sort out the letting agent details. She had offered the flat as furnished, but she needed to pack up her personal things, which she boxed and stored in her parents' garage in Frome, just outside of Bath.

'I'm going home,' she told her mother over coffee in their living room. 'Back to Blue Sands. I felt like I needed a break and Joan offered me a job in the shop.'

'Won't that be strange?' Lisa said. 'You were a teenager when you worked in there before.'

'I know. It'll probably be a bit weird at first, but once I get used to it, it'll be like the old days.'

'Well, have a nice time. Say hello to the place. While your father and I have been happy here these last five years, we still miss it. It has a certain … magic.'

Grace smiled. 'I will,' she said.

It felt like a prison break when she got a taxi to Temple Meads Station and bought a train ticket to Penzance. June 1st, the first day of summer. It was pouring with rain, but Grace hadn't been so excited in years. With her suitcase in the luggage storage overhead and an agreement on a chalet just back from the beach for a three-month rental, Grace felt like the world was beginning to knit itself back together. Ten years in Bristol hadn't been all bad, but as the train pulled out of the station, she felt excited to be going, rather than sad to leave.

On my way, she messaged Joan.

I'll be waiting at Penzance, came the reply.

Just like old times. Drinks on the beach, coffee in the café … thanks Joanie. You've saved my life.

I just helped you to save it yourself. It's raining here, by the way.

Ha! Nothing ever changes.

The reply took a little longer to come than Grace might have expected. Perhaps Joan was in the toilet or busy with something.

No, nothing.

Joanie … are you okay?

Of course. Why?

I just thought … never mind.

Can't wait to see you, Graceful.

You too.

6

REUNION

Despite it being perhaps the first train Grace had ever caught from Temple Meads that was officially on time, the journey down to Penzance seemed to take an age. Once they were through Plymouth the journey became one of frequent stops at little Cornish towns, many of which Grace and Joan had painted red over wild weekends of drinking and clubbing, back in their carefree teens when the responsibilities of adulthood had felt like a million years away. There were star shapes they had gouged out of a hotel's flowerbed, a weathervane stolen from a town centre monument … there was the boot of a police car Grace had woken up in—to the bemused looks of a pair of local bobbies—after Joan had managed to pop the lid with a penknife. And in between the wild times there had been warm summer days wandering desolate beaches, writing their names in pristine sand, beers and burgers around stone-walled barbeque pits on late summer evenings, and local sea shanties sung late into the night.

And then Grace had gone to university in Bristol, and everything had changed. For a few years she had maintained a regular summer visit, but when she was twenty-three, her parents had moved up to Frome, partly to be nearer to her, and partly because after thirty years living in Cornwall they wanted a change of scenery.

Grace understood. But only after her own visits to Blue Sands declined to a couple of biennial weeks, did she realise how much she missed the pretty little cove and its crescent of welcoming sand. Even the Hill of Suffering had grown to be remembered with fondness, the dark nights of climbing up from the pub in the pouring rain, had become a quirk of country life rather than something to dread after a night of pleasurable drinking in the pub.

I'm going to do it this time, she messaged Joan just after the train had pulled out of Redruth. *I'm going to ride it, and you're going to walk alongside me. Well, not quite alongside, just a little bit back.*

The reply took a while to come, making Grace wonder whether Joan was having second thoughts.

Sounds like a plan.

Are you all right?

Yeah, great. Can't wait to see you!

It was just a little eager. Not like Joan at all. There was definitely something up.

An hour later, just after seven p.m., the train pulled into Penzance station. Grace had been dozing, idly dreaming about a time she and Joan had gone out on the lash in Newquay and woken up in a field of cows. Joan had been using a cow pat as a pillow. Luckily it had been dry. They'd walked across fields until they found themselves in a quiet little village, where they'd got a massive fry-up and large mugs of coffee. They'd spent the rest of the day lounging about on the little strip of sand, eating ice-creams and talking about nothing. In a souvenir shop just back from the beach Grace had bought a little dream catcher decorated with shells, which she had hung over her bed right through university.

She had a smile on her face as she sat up just in time to see the PENZANCE sign slide gently past her window as the train came to a stop.

She peered out of the window, looking for Joan, but there was no sign of her friend. Grabbing her suitcase, she hauled it down the aisle and out onto the platform. A few commuters were heading swiftly for the exit stairs. A young student-type was trying to escape a smothering embrace from his parents. A mother pushed a pram with one hand while holding the hand of a little girl with the other.

'Hi, Graceful. Told you I'd be waiting.'

'Joanie? Joan—' Grace spun around. Her jaw dropped. Joan had never been slim like Grace, but age had filled Joan out. Remembering how they had used to gorge on the ice-creams on a quiet day left Grace unsurprised, but the wheelchair from which Joan looked up was unexpected, to say the least.

'What happened? Your tongue got caught under the train?'

All Grace could do was stare. 'I didn't … I didn't know.'

Joan shrugged, then wheeled herself a couple of feet forward. She fixed Grace with a warm look, even as she gave a sad smile. 'I know you didn't. That's because I didn't tell you.'

The joyful homecoming Grace had expected evaporated in front of her eyes like smoke puffing from the train's exhaust. With tears in her eyes she reached forward and pulled Joan into a hug.

'Damn it, why didn't you tell me?'

'You had cancer and you didn't tell me?'

Joan sighed. 'I had a tumour in my lower spine,' she said, stirring her coffee as they sat in a café across from the station. A drop splashed onto the floral tablecloth, which Joan swiped up with a finger before it could sink in. 'It was hurting like hell to sit, for no particular reason. You know me, I was never one to be out swimming laps of the bay like you did, so there wasn't any cause for it. The doctor ran some tests, then they did a scan which showed the tumour. The doctor said I'd caught it a month before it would have been inoperable. The surgery saved me, but I lost the use of my legs.'

'I'm so pissed,' Grace said, sobbing into a tissue. 'I can't believe you didn't tell me. We're best friends. All through it you were messaging me like everything was fine.'

Joan grinned, then reached across and slapped Grace's forearm. 'Will you stop bloody crying? I'm fine. Well, more or less. I'm not climbing cliff paths anymore but I'm still getting around, still running the café so Mum can go off to her flower arranging classes and cream tea lunches. I can still read a book and drink a pint, and give my best friend advice on her pathetic love life.'

'You should have said!'

'Yeah, and then you would have come swanning back down to Blue Sands to look after me, when the last thing I wanted was sympathy.' Joan slapped the top of her thigh. 'You know what this feels like? A second chance. I stared death in the face, and I know what it felt like to be close to the end. I've never lived life better.'

Grace scowled. 'I'm still angry with you.'

'Oh, shut up and eat your scone. You've got room for a lot more than I have. What would you have done if I'd told you?'

'I'd have been by your side.'

Joan shook her head. 'I've missed you since the day you left Blue Sands, Graceful, and I dreamed of the day you came back. But, I didn't want it to be because I needed you. I wanted it to be because you needed me.'

'I need you.'

Joan grinned, licked the tip of her finger, held it up and made a hissing sound. 'Objective achieved. Can we stop talking about me now?'

Grace shook her head. 'No! You had cancer and you didn't tell me. It'll be days before I stop being angry with you.'

'Are you going to throw a tray of coffee over me?'

Grace grimaced. 'Ouch. Low blow.'

'Ha, that would be total discrimination. Do you think they'll give you an ASBO? Are you even allowed to visit me? Aren't you tagged or something?' She twisted the chair so the footrest nudged Grace's leg. 'Go on, let me see your ankles.'

'I'm not tagged. They didn't seem to mind. In the great scheme of things, I don't think I'm considered that desperate a criminal. As long as I gave the police a forwarding address and phone number, they said it was all good.'

'Perhaps the PC had the hots for you.'

Grace rolled her eyes. 'I don't think so. It was a woman.'

Joan punched her armrest. 'Will you stop discriminating? I'm offended by default. What if I told you I was a lesbian too?'

'Are you? Is that something else you haven't told me?'

Joan laughed. 'No. I'm fully active on Tinder. In the restricted access section. She gave the chair a shake. Quite a fetish, these things. You wouldn't believe the weirdoes who contact me. One guy wanted to know the brand name and model number.'

'What did you do?'

'I swiped left.'

'Is that good or bad?'

Joan rolled her eyes. 'God, you're so nineties. We'll have to sort you out. Come on, let's get out of here and get back to Blue Sands. How long are you going to leave me standing here?'

'You're not—'

'It was a joke, Graceful. Come on. I've got one of those nifty cars with the steering wheel controls. It's a total trip.'

Being disabled hadn't impacted the violence of Joan's driving. With her heart in her mouth, Grace hung on to the armrest for dear life as Joan hacked them through the worst of Cornwall's country lanes at a harrowing speed, working the car from a system of buttons fitted to the steering wheel.

'Wow, forgot about that pothole,' Joan said, as they bumped through half a mine shaft dug out of the middle of the road with such violence that Grace bounced up out of the seat.

'So, what's changed?' Grace gasped, hoping the distraction of conversation might encourage Joan to slow down. 'How's the Low Anchor? Still run by Dawn and Craig?'

Joan shook her head as they came to a straight section

where Grace was able to catch her breath. 'Nope. Remember that stuck up Gomersall girl? Taylor?'

'Tay Gomersall, her of the weird name. Ha, yeah, I remember. A few years below us at school.'

'Well, Craig got caught shagging her out by the Mourning Lady a couple of summers back. One of the Thompson boys was out there walking his dog.' Joan grinned. 'Man, the gossip was going off for a while. Anyway, long story short, Craig and Dawn got divorced, they sold the pub, and Craig shacked up with Taylor in one of those council flats up on Black Rock Drive. Got himself a job as a lifeguard, acting all young like.'

'Wasn't he like, old?'

'Forties. Yeah. Proper made a tit of himself. Anyway, he got sacked because some tourist kid got in trouble in the undertow last September. Craig couldn't get to him, and a couple of locals had to pull him out. Lost his job, Taylor dumped him, and they both ended up leaving. Last I heard she was at nursing college and he was running a bar in Plymouth.'

'Wow, I'm totally out of the loop, it looks like. Who owns the pub now?'

Joan grimaced. 'Ah, um … Daniel. Um, Daniel Woakes.'

Grace felt like someone had slapped her from the inside, making her cheeks smart from the inside out.

'Dan? You've got to be having a laugh. As in my ex-boyfriend, Dan?'

Joan took both hands off the wheel long enough to make quotation marks in the air. 'Your teenage love, yeah.'

'Please hold the wheel.'

'Ha, sure.' Joan grabbed the wheel just in time to hack them round a blind corner. As the hedgerow opened out,

Grace half expected to find a tractor coming the other way, but luckily the road was clear.

'For your information, he wasn't my teenage love.'

'You just shagged him a few times?'

'It was more than that.'

'But less than total infatuation?'

'Somewhere in the middle. Is it going to be awkward me showing up? We didn't part on the best of terms.'

'You dumped him, didn't you?'

'We broke up. There's a difference. I went to university, he stayed here. God, we were only teenagers.'

Joan grinned. 'Weren't those the days?'

'We had some good times.'

'We had a lot of good times. But, since you were asking, I'm not sure about awkward, but I wouldn't go expecting locals' rates. It's been a while, but he might be a bit salty about everything.' Joan leaned across and nudged Grace's arm, making the car swerve dangerously close to a thorny hedge. 'After all, you went off to the big city to go to university and make something of yourself, leaving him behind in a nowhere seaside village.'

'And look how that worked out. It turns out a degree in history is only good enough to wait tables, and meanwhile, my uneducated, country bumpkin ex becomes the owner of the most popular pub in the area.'

'Don't worry, there are a few nerds from school still around. I'm sure we can find someone who'll let you play the sympathy card.'

'Shut up!'

As she hacked into another blind corner, Joan had tears in her eyes and a wide grin on her face.

'It's so good to have you back, Graceful. Here we are. Just as you remember.'

7

RETURN

BLUE SANDS WAS SPLIT INTO TWO PARTS. UPPER BLUE Sands was a little village a mile from the beach, set back from the hill's crest in a flat hollow surrounding a church, apparently because a long, long time ago that would have made it hidden from Vikings cruising up and down the coast. Blue Sands Cove, on the other hand, was the name given to the cluster of houses and businesses catering to tourists which surrounded the beach itself, a flat stretch of golden sand with a paved promenade a quarter of a mile long. Back in the valley and along the hills that rose to either side, where the beach was cut off by a pair of jutting headlands, a number of expensive holiday homes poked up out of the scattering of woodland, ensuring that all the best views of the cove, besides the one from the road, were exclusive to toffs from up country.

'We'll do a quick swing through the cove just so you can remember what it looks like,' Joan said, as they came around a corner to face the upper stretch of the Hill of Suffering. It looked steeper than Grace remembered, dropping seemingly sheer towards the beach before hitting the annoying cutback a third of the way up which was famous for derailing cycling attempts. In fact, seeing it with her teenage years far behind her, she could understand why it was common to see taxis ferrying people up and down in midsummer, even though no local would be seen dead in one. The thought of trying to walk it made the back of her neck tickle.

Locals joked that the cutback was to slow drivers coming down, and that the gate directly opposite the road had the outlines of dozens who had failed, but the geological truth was that just through the gate was a lump of jutting granite ten feet high that the road builders had not bothered to move, perhaps out of laziness or lack of leadership. And now, like one of those annoying bumps in a straight line caused by a nock in a ruler, the road wound out around the corner of the field in which the rock stood, before cutting back around, dropping again towards the beach in the steepest section, and then swinging around a corner to bring the promenade and the shoreline into view.

'You remember the Singing Rock?' Joan said, slowing the car as they reached the bottom of the upper section of the hill, so that they could see through the overgrown gateway. 'Every night, wasn't it? On the lash, we'd be in there, climbing up that thing, singing like muppets until the dawn.'

'Or the cops came out.'

'That was once. Only once. And it was Julia's dad, so he just told us to shut up and go home.'

'He actually joined us for a song.'

Joan laughed. 'Couldn't do that now, with people filming everything on smartphones. Can't have any fun anymore, can you?'

'Do the kids still climb it?'

Joan shook her head. 'The farmer, Bill Clifford, he put

a padlock on the gate and some barbed wire over the top. Kids were going in there, getting hammered, and leaving all their crap behind.'

'We used to stuff ours in the beach bins.'

'The council took them away. Fascists.'

Grace shook her head. 'Not like it used to be, is it?'

Joan sighed and moved the car on, cutting around the jutting field hedge of the Singing Rock, past the turning that led to the coast road heading south, down the steepest section of the hill and around the corner at the bottom.

'Some things change,' Joan said, grinning, 'but some things never change.'

Grace smiled at the promenade stretching away in front of them. 'Just how I remember.'

The tide was high, gentle breakers lapping at a pristine stretch of sand below a jumble of rocks. Along the promenade that followed the line of the road and on the beach, people strolled, walked their dogs, stood talking in groups as the sun hung low in the sky. Just behind the promenade, halfway along a line of small shops, lights shone from the windows of the Low Anchor, the cove's most popular pub and site of much teenage mischief.

'Do you want to stop for a pint?' Joan said. 'Mum's cooking dinner, but we can squeeze in half an hour. I did say you're staying at mine tonight? I'm not having you alone in that chalet on your first night back.'

Grace laughed. 'Just let me get a little sleep, though. I couldn't sleep on the train. I was too excited. I think I'll pass on the pub, though. I'm not ready to see Daniel right now. I'd rather build up to it.'

'Gotcha. We'll do a quick turn of the beachfront then head up. Don't worry, Dad's got plenty of beers in.'

As they drove past the pub, weaving around several cars which had disobeyed traffic rules to park along the promenade—another thing that hadn't changed—Grace glanced up at the windows, wondering if she'd catch a glimpse of Daniel. She saw an elderly couple sat at one window table, but of her ex-boyfriend there was no sign. Probably just as well. While ten years had eased the pain of it, Grace had glossed over their breakup for Joan's benefit. She wasn't sure she'd ever got over the handsome surfer who had been the first person to capture her heart. She still thought of him often, even though they'd had no contact since her first departure from Blue Sands. She was glad he had done well for himself. She only wished she could say the same.

'Seen enough for one day? I reckon it's dinner time. Mum and Dad can't wait to see you again.'

'Sounds good.'

As they reached the end of the promenade, where Joan did a U-turn in the gravel track where locals took boats down on to the beach, Grace tried again to get a glimpse of Daniel through the pub windows.

I'm sorry I broke your heart, she thought, as the car sped past, Joan accelerating far harder than necessary into the Hill of Suffering's bottom corner. *But if it makes you feel better, I broke my own at the same time.*

8

OLD THINGS AND MEMORIES

HOME.

It felt crazy to be back, but in a way it felt right. Blue Sands was where Grace had grown up, and for all its faults, nothing made her feel alive more than the sight of the sun peeking above the hills in the early morning, the crash of the sea on the shore, the call of the herring gulls as they terrorised some poor unsuspecting tourist.

All these years away, trying to dig herself some kind of life in Bristol, yet it took barely a few hours back in the old village before she felt layers of stress lifting off her shoulders like departing birds.

Dinner with Joan's parents, Ron and Belinda Turner, was a quirky affair. Known for their summer parties back in the day, the Turners had settled down, and by the end of a hearty roast dinner only three bottles of wine had been drunk between them. Grace and Joan sat up talking long after Joan's parents had gone to bed, but while ten years ago they might have pulled an all-nighter, now Grace was done by midnight, and let Joan show her down the hall to a guest bedroom. They hugged each other good night, then with a smile, Joan asked Grace to wheel her down to her own bedroom and help her get into bed, even though Joan grumpily insisted she had a method of rolling sideways out of the chair which really didn't require any assistance. It was a sobering moment, and it was a long time before she could sleep, as she stared at the ceiling, thinking about how much had changed.

Nursing less of a hangover than she might have expected, Grace was up before everyone else the next morning, and after leaving a short note on the kitchen counter, headed out for a walk around the village.

On the surface, it looked much the same. There was scaffolding up the church tower, and two new houses on a corner where an old farm shed had once stood, rotting away in a field, but most of the buildings remained unchanged. A few new cars stood in the driveways of houses that had once belonged to friends, while the grass was long and unkempt in a few others. The Whelans, whose twin boys Grace had gone to playschool with, had gone, their big house on the corner next to the newsagent with a FOR SALE sign poking out of the lawn at an angle. And the old Spar where Grace and Joan had once been caught trying to shoplift Mars Bars—a literal slap on the wrist by the local copper might not have derailed their teenage years of mayhem but had certainly turned them away from a life of crime—was now a sparkling boutique café, with signboards outside offering soy lattes, as well as one nostalgic throwback called The Old Heart Attack, a full fat, full sugar monstrosity topped with handmade marshmallows, local cream and chocolate from trees grown in the Eden Project. Grace made a note to check it out; if Joan was a frequent customer it would explain why she had filled out a little.

Otherwise, the village looked much as it always had.

Grace walked the length of the small high street, then looped back through the interlinking residential streets that made up a de facto estate, to where the old combined village library and museum stood, a small two-storey building perched on the edge of a hill. It had been owned by the Davis family back in the day, Frank being the drama teacher at Grace and Joan's school, and his wife, Tina, a school counsellor. Their son, Paul, had been in Grace's form, a quiet boy always with his head in a book, too boring for any of the local bullies to take notice.

As Grace paused to look at the view of the valley beyond the car park to the library's rear, through the windows she noticed someone inside, already stacking books onto shelves. In case the person wondered what she was doing, she quickly made herself scarce, heading back up the street, cutting through a series of alleys between the cluster of houses, and then walking up to the top of Melrose Hill, where a small picnic area stood on a flattened area at the top of a field, with a panoramic view of Blue Sands Cove below.

To the north, the jutting headland rose to a small peak then flattened out, dipping back towards the sea, where a small, automatic lighthouse was built on the last buttress above the water, a rock known as Blue Point. To the south, the cliffs stretched further out into the bay, ending in an inaccessible lump known as Sharker's Rock. It was where older men went to fish, or brave local kids to jump off the rocks into the rising swell of the Atlantic. From her vantage point, Grace could see the grey rolls of swell breaking over the rocks, sending up showers of spray.

Closer, the gentle curve of sand and the promenade at the back of the foreshore were just visible above the slope of the field. The sea was at low tide, revealing a stretch of dark orange sand scattered with patches of seaweed-covered rocks. A couple of people walked among them, occasionally bending to peer into rock pools, while a pair of dogs raced each other along the glistening sand nearby.

From here, most of the houses and shops back from the shore were hidden out of view, but the roof of the Low Anchor was just visible. Grace gave a little shake of her head. She hadn't given it a thought that she might bump into Daniel Woakes again. He had always loved Blue Sands in a way that had almost made Grace jealous, but surely by now he would have been off in the world, making something of himself?

She walked back out of the picnic area to the road. Peering down the steep slope of Melrose Hill, Grace grimaced. While she could handle the down, she didn't fancy the walk back up to Joan's place so early in the morning. She needed a few days to adjust. Bristol, while hilly in places, had nothing on this monster.

When she returned to Joan's parents' place, she found the family up and about. Ron was sitting in the car, just about to leave for work, and he wound down the window to wish her good morning, before heading off to Penzance and the office job he had been doing for as long as Grace could remember. In the kitchen, Grace and her mother were arguing flippantly over politics and newspapers, with Joan's mother suggesting that they ban a certain tabloid from the shop because of its treatment of the Royal Family.

'But all the builders buy that one,' Joan said. 'And the builders buy most of the pasties. We'd cut our morning income by half.'

'Well, I want it put at the back,' Belinda said, putting the coffee cup on its saucer with a soft clink.

'Morning, Grace,' Joan said, looking up with a grin. 'Are you ready for your first day? We'll ease you back in with washing the salt crust off the windows, then we need you to unblock the toilet. We leave in fifteen minutes. Okay?' As Grace stared, openmouthed, Joan cackled with laughter. 'Only having a laugh. We'll give you a few days to get settled. Saturday okay? You can help with the early season rush. It's supposed to be sunny this weekend. Fancy that?'

Grace smiled. 'Sounds good.'

'But the toilet is blocked. Some kid stuffed an entire bog roll down it. We're going to draw straws on who has to do the plunging.'

'I've done worse,' Grace said. 'You should have seen the toilets at Jones's on a Sunday morning. Someone stuffed an umbrella down one once. Bent it right around the U-Bend. Had to call out a specialist plumber because the building is listed and you have to be really careful about not damaging anything. We had to call out this girl who'd been on the TV. My manager was moaning about the cost for days.'

Joan shook her head. 'Mental. Those bankers let their hair down on a weekend, I take it?'

'Oh, yeah.'

Belinda offered Grace a seat and she got stuck into some breakfast. Losing her mobility hadn't affected Joan's appetite, and Grace realised she was starving too. Belinda had made American-style pancakes just for the occasion, and Grace found herself three-deep before she realised. She turned down the offer of a fourth, but Joan suddenly lifted a hand, waving it about as though to attract attention.

'God, I almost forgot. Seeing you stuffing your face reminded me. I have something for you out in the shed.'

'Really? What?'

'Your bike.'

45

'My … bike?'

'Yeah. When your parents sold up, your dad did a garage sale. Mum and me went over to pick through your old stuff.'

Grace nodded. 'I remember. You said you bought my old Take That CDs and threw them in the trash.'

'I lied. I gave them to the Oxfam shop in Truro. Last time I looked they were still there.'

Grace sighed. 'Dad was so gutted about flogging off my stuff. I told him it was fine, but he felt so guilty about it. Not like I had anywhere to put it, and I was never one to look back. I'd already taken everything I needed.'

'Well, I got your bike.'

'My old racer.' Grace could barely bring herself to believe it. She had a newer one in Bristol, but the racing bike her parents had bought her for her fourteenth birthday had been the reason she had got into road biking. She had once cycled all the way to Plymouth during the summer holiday, the bike gliding easily along the open roads, as fast as some of the cars.

Joan lifted an eyebrow. 'No, not that one. Johnny Bellow's son Sam got that one, then promptly crashed it halfway down Melrose Hill the following week.'

'So … you don't mean—'

Joan gave a slow nod. 'Yeah, I do. The bike you're going to climb the Hill of Suffering on, and which you have to do because I'm in a wheelchair and I've requested it. The challenge is laid down, Graceful. Do you accept?'

Grace stared at the fork in her hand, a lump of pancake hanging off the end. With a soft plop, it fell off and landed in a puddle of honey.

'My pink BMX,' she said.

9

J'S SURF SHACK

JOAN AND BELINDA DROPPED GRACE AND HER OLD BIKE off at her chalet on their way to the café. With a warm morning sun just beating off the chill from a breeze coming in off the sea, she left her suitcase out of sight behind a large flower pot beside the door, then rode up the street to the local letting agency office and collected the keys.

The chalet was part of a terrace of five properties set into the hill on the southern edge of the cove, and from the window of the little kitchen there was a narrow view of the beach between the houses lining the seafront. On a budget, Grace had got the best she could afford, but the little square of garden at the back was so close to the hill as to be almost permanently in shadow. However, with a small living room and kitchen downstairs and a bedroom and bathroom upstairs, it was perfectly adequate for her needs.

Wanting as clean a slate as she could get, she had packed only the one suitcase, stuffing it full of summer clothes and what remained of her beachwear. Otherwise she had some makeup and toiletries, her phone (no reception), her little laptop (no internet), and a handful of books she had bought in the shop at Temple Meads. The Blue Sands Café, owned by Belinda and mostly run by Joan, could only give her a few hours of work five days a week, but it gave Grace just enough to get by while leaving her time to relax and maybe think about the direction of her life. Hell, after years of treading water in Bristol, she owed herself a break.

She leaned the pink BMX against the chalet's white-washed outer wall, smiling at the memories it brought back. Then, thinking better of it, she used a padlock Joan had given her to lock it to the front gate, in case some opportunistic twelve-year-old came past and fancied a freebie. Clean and in good condition, it might still appeal to a certain demographic, even if the half-removed BMX label that Grace had never been able to fully get rid of made it a throwback to a past age.

Then, after unpacking her suitcase, hanging her clothes in a clean, lavender-smelling wardrobe and arranging the rest of her things on various dresser tops and in drawers, she went out for a walk.

It was still only a little after ten in the morning and Blue Sands Cove was just waking up. As was the nature of many Cornish villages, at least half of the houses were holiday homes rarely used outside August, so the handful of narrow streets was mostly deserted. She greeted a boy delivering newspapers, and paused to watch a little local bus trundle along the road behind the promenade, its only passengers a kid wearing headphones and an old lady wrestling with a broadsheet newspaper.

Across the road from the promenade, t-shirt and shorts-clad staff from several surf rental shops were setting out signboards and gear. On the promenade, a younger generation of local surfers was already sitting on the edge of the seawall, perusing the low breakers rolling in against the shore. For a few years in her teens, Grace had been among them. While Joan had liked the beach but not the water, Grace's mid-teens had brought a brief obsession with the waves that had even won her a couple of local prizes. However, like most of her possessions, she had given her parents permission to sell her surfboard, and with ten years having passed since the last time she hit the waves, she wasn't sure her body could still take it.

Today, however, with a gentle two-foot break massaging the shore, was a good time to try. She walked up to the first shop she saw with an OPEN sign and went inside. Immediately, the waxy scent of the place, the stacks of boards and wetsuits, and the surfing video playing quietly on a TV hanging from the ceiling took her back. For a few moments Grace just stood there, remembering better, more carefree days.

'Help you?' came a voice from a corner. A sales counter plastered with brand logo stickers, was half-obscured by leaning boards. A young man wearing a Stone Age sweatshirt stood behind it. His matted hair was bleached blond, his smile relaxed.

Grace met his eyes and frowned. 'Don't I know you from somewhere?'

The man pouted, shaking his head. 'Maybe. Dunno. You local?'

'I was. My name's Grace Clelland. I used to live up in the village.'

The young man came out from behind the counter and stood with his arms folded, watching her. 'Ah, I remember you. You were Dan Woakes's girl.'

At the sudden recognition, Grace started. 'Well, I don't think I'd quite say that,' she said. 'It was only a month. Perhaps a summer.'

The man smiled again. 'Long enough. You don't know me? Jason. Jason King. I was a couple of years below you. I used to help out in the school library.'

Grace stared. 'Jason? The nerd Jason? Weren't you thin?'

Jason laughed. 'Filled out a bit in my late teens. Got a laser job on my eyes and got into the boards a bit. The sea water cleared up the spots like nothing else.' He shrugged. 'Still read, you know, when the surf's flat. You look … toned.'

'Ah, thanks. Spinning.'

'Spinning? What's that? Some kind of biking, isn't it?'

'Yeah, it's when the bike wheel only moves when you pedal. It doesn't free wheel. So you have to keep moving.'

Jason laughed. 'Sounds weird. Better to go get a ride outside, isn't it?'

Grace smiled. 'Yeah, I think it is.'

'Take on that hill. Gonna try? Got a race this August Bank Holiday. First one to the top gets the new surf club cat named after them. Been getting some practice in, gonna have a go. Reckon Jason fits.'

'A cat called Jason?'

'Catamaran.'

'Oh.'

'Yeah, they're gonna use it for surf lifesaving training offshore.'

'Sounds interesting.'

'Gonna have a crack?'

'A crack at what?'

'The race. Gonna be a few celebs there. Can't have one of them winning it, can we? Gotta be a local. All that spinning, reckon you can do an uphill?'

It was something Grace had been planning to challenge herself with over the course of the summer.

However, she had planned to cycle alone with Joan walking alongside to provide the benchmark speed. Now that couldn't happen, she hadn't made any decision on what to do, but Jason was staring at her with a small smile on his face, as though daring her to accept the challenge.

She smiled. 'I think Grace is a pretty good name for a catamaran,' she said. 'I'll be there. And in the meantime, I'd like to rent a surfboard.'

Jason nodded. 'Nothing like a bit of cross training. You gonna head out to the rock?'

'Which rock?'

'Sharker's. Got rollers coming in. A few of the lads are gonna take a boat out this morning, wait for the big guys. Should be epic. I'd be there but I've gotta work.'

'Ah, I'm a bit out of practice, so I was thinking more to just hit up the regular surf. You know, over on the beach there.'

Jason frowned. 'But you're a local.'

'So?'

'Locals can't be seen in there.'

'Why not?'

'That's tourist surf, that is.'

Grace laughed. She had once shared Jason's opinion. Times had changed, though. She had been a long time away.

'Is there any way for me to not look local?'

Jason frowned for a moment, then lifted a hand and clicked his fingers with a dry crack.

'Got a suit over here,' he said, going to a corner and poking about. 'You're what, five six?'

'That's right.'

Jason held up a bright sky blue wetsuit and turned it around. On the back, in huge white letters, it read, RENTED FROM J'S SURF SHACK.

'Can see it from the beach,' Jason said. 'I'll let you use it for free if you like. With this on, no one'll know you're local. Helps with the rep.'

Grace grimaced. If you could see the writing on the suit from the beach, you would be able to see it from the Low Anchor's windows.

'Do you have a helmet I can wear?' she asked. 'Just to make sure no one can recognise me? Or a mask?'

Jason frowned. 'Swell's only about two foot. Not gonna hurt yourself in that.'

'But just in case?'

'Don't be a wuss.'

'I'd really prefer it.'

Jason shook his head. 'People'll think I'm trying to fleece you. Look, I'll give you half rates on a day's rental for the board, and the suit is free. And I'll throw in a can of Coke. Can't say better than that, can I?'

Grace stared at the suit with its gleaming white letters that looked freshly printed. 'What's the chance of sea mist coming in this morning?' she asked.

Jason smiled. 'None.'

10

BREAKERS

No one heckled her as she walked down to the beach with the rental board under her arm, but she caught a couple of grins from dog walkers as she reached the shoreline.

'Good morning,' one young guy called as he tossed a stick for an eager Labrador. 'Down on holiday?'

'Something like that,' Grace answered, ignoring the smirk behind his words as she strapped the leash to her ankle. From the shoreline, the breakers looked even smaller than they had from outside J's Surf Shack, tiny, feeble little things perhaps not even strong enough to lift the board. As she moved the board out into the water, she realised the only other people in the sea were two groups of kids playing in the shallows. A couple held up polystyrene boards to the breakers, others tossed a beach ball back and forth.

At least no one will recognise me.

She had soon pushed the board out to waist deep. At low tide, the beach was a gentle slope, and already she had gone beyond the break line. Feeling like an amateur rather than someone who had once dragged herself out of bed at six o'clock to catch a few waves before school, she pushed the board back until she was just inside the first gentle breakers. Then, climbing on, she began to paddle for the swell.

From flat on the board, the wave rose behind her, pushing her up out of the water. Grace paddled hard, feeling the old thrill of catching on to a wave. As the water took her, she laid her hands flat and tried to flip herself up into a standing position, only to find that her body's old flexibility had deserted her.

She made it halfway to her knees, before overbalancing and falling sideways off the board. For a moment freezing, salty water filled her senses, then her bum bumped against the sand and she stood up, the water reaching just above her thighs.

Nearby, something was buzzing in the water. Grace turned to see a small motorboat speeding out from the beach's northern end, angling across the shore towards Sharker's Rock at the far southern headland, where proper rollers had begun to pound. A couple of men she couldn't recognise over the distance lifted their hands to wave.

'Nice break!' someone shouted, accompanied by a cackle of laughter from the others. Grace scowled, tugging the leash line to pull the board back to her. More determined than ever, she turned the board around and pushed it back out into the surf. The motorboat was past her now, but up along the promenade, a few people had stopped to watch. Or was it her imagination?

Trying not to feel a prickle of embarrassment, she paddled onto the next swell, another two-foot monster which would have failed to threaten the defenses of a child's sandcastle. She felt the board catch, pushed herself up, managed to hold a position at one knee for a few seconds, then fell sideways into the water. This time, she was barely submerged before she hit sand.

She was catching funny looks from the children further up the beach. They were only little, she realised now, pre-school age. Their parents watched from the sand nearby.

Grace wanted one more go before she gave up. Turning the board around, she climbed on top and began to paddle, only to feel the board's fin scraping the sand beneath her. Glancing back at the foreshore, it appeared at least a dozen people were now watching her from the promenade.

The swell rose behind her. Determined to prove a point, or at least provide some entertainment, Grace paddled hard, aiming to catch the little wave at the exact point of breaking, and ride it serenely into the beach. As it caught her, however, she tilted the board too straight. The wave broke behind her, pointing her straight down. She gamely tried to stand, but as the board's tip hit the sand it flipped her forward. For a brief moment she was airborne, arms flailing, then she was crashing into the shallows.

She rolled over as delicate little waves lapped at her body. The traitorous board bumped gently against her leg as she looked up into the face of a child clutching a beach ball.

'Are you all right?'

Joan shook her head. 'Are you out of your mind?' she asked, sitting in her wheelchair across the table from Grace. 'I mean, there's not even enough swell for the sponge boarders to play, and you went out there in full gear?'

Grace shrugged and licked her ice-cream. 'It looked better from the beach.'

'You've been away too long.'

Across on the promenade, a family strolled past, buckets and spades in hand. A toddler's arm lifted to single out Grace.

'Mummy, there's the surfing lady,' the little boy said. 'She's funny.'

'Go on, give them a wave,' Joan said, trying not to laugh. 'Less than a day you've been back and you're already a celebrity.'

Grace gave the family a quick thumbs-up, resulting in laughter from the two children. She pushed her sunglasses further up her nose as they walked on, wishing she'd pressed Jason harder for the rental of a mask.

'At least Jason didn't charge me for the board's broken tip,' Grace said. 'He told me he'd had twenty customers already that morning. Someone even bought a board. He said I could keep the wetsuit if I wanted.'

'He's a good lad. Good mates with Daniel, too. He'll know you're back by the end of the day for sure.'

'If he didn't see me himself.' Grace sighed. 'I don't think there's much chance of igniting that old flame.'

Joan grimaced. 'Ah, Graceful, there's something—'

The café door opened and Belinda leaned out. 'Joan, we've got the pasty guy on the phone. Can you handle tomorrow's order please?'

Joan gave Grace a regretful smile. 'Work calls,' she said. 'I'll see you later. What are you going to do for the rest of the day?'

'Sit on my patio and read a book.'

'Ah, staying out of trouble?'

'Something like that.'

After Joan went back inside, Grace finished her ice-cream and walked along the promenade. It seemed that her brief, embarrassing surf had made her a minor celebrity, with a couple of strangers wishing her uncharacteristically jovial hellos.

At the end of the promenade, she took the little bridge that led over the stream gurgling down from the upper valley and walked onto the beach. It was nearly lunchtime, but the beach was fairly quiet, most people still at work or school. Grace wandered around the foreshore for a while, before taking a path leading up the cliff to the south. In a hollow set back from the beach stood the surf club, a small stone building surrounded by a grassy bank. Only members had keys, but there was a notice board outside which Grace paused to peruse.

Jason was right. Over the last weekend of August, there was a beach gala, including a number of events such as the Melrose Hill Bicycle Race, a team tug-of-war, a life-saving competition and a paddle board race. Most of the events were open only to teams or surf club members, but Grace signed her name under an open list for the bicycle race, and then, as an afterthought, for the mixed surfing competition.

With ten years of inactivity behind her, she wouldn't have a chance against some of the local kids who dedicated their lives to the waves, but it would give her a chance to make up for the morning's embarrassment. She would be sure to ask Jason to keep the wetsuit back for the occasion.

'I'll show you,' she muttered with a smile.

11

OLD FRIENDS

THE CHALET'S TINY GARDEN COLLECTED THE SUN FROM just after three p.m. until five, which was long enough for Grace to settle with a pot of tea, some biscuits she had picked up on her walk home, and a book. With her phone unable to get a signal down in the cove, she was entirely free from distractions, barring the occasional call of a gull which came to perch on the chalet's roof in hope of some crumbs.

Just after seven o'clock, by which time she had moved to the sofa in her small living room, a tremulous ringing came from a cupboard in the hallway. Narrowly avoiding spilling her most recent cup of tea, Grace discovered she had a landline. When she tentatively answered, Joan's voice explained she had got the number from the letting agent. They agreed to meet for fish'n'chips on the promenade at eight o'clock.

It was certainly a sobering moment and a reminder of how things had changed to see Joan wheeling her chair along the promenade. As Grace jumped up from the bench where she was waiting and hurried to help, Joan waved her away, telling her, 'It's the only exercise I get these days.'

On Grace's recommendation, they went to a popular place just back from the main road called Haddock Enough Yet?, which hadn't changed much since their teenage years, even if the owner, Gerry, had now retired to a villa in the south of France and been replaced behind the fryers by his son Brian, whom Grace remembered from a couple of years above her at school. The fish'n'chips smelled as good as ever, and the only change appeared to be in the portion sizes ('gotta match the competition') and the replacement of old newspaper with greaseproof ('sod the government; they have no idea of taste').

They took their warm, greasy bundles back to the promenade. To Grace's surprise Joan suggested they eat on the beach, and pointed to a disabled access ramp nearby.

Realising that the slope was inappropriately steep, Grace took the handles and lowered Joan down backwards to the bottom of the ramp where it ended at a patch of rocks which was beach in name only. She then hauled Joan's chair a few metres through dry sand until they came to a small patch clear of stones.

'Right, tip me over.'

'Are you sure?'

'You think I'd make you haul me down here just to sit in this stupid chair? Don't worry, I'm used to this kind of thing. Haven't been on the beach in years, though. Probably not since before the operation. Mum doesn't have the shoulders for it.'

'If you really want.'

'Just lean me sideways and brace me so I don't end up going down face first.'

It wasn't easy, but with a bit of maneuvering, Grace

was able to get Joan out of the chair and prop her up against a rock.

'Just like old times, Graceful,' Joan said, brushing sand off her thighs.

'Yeah,' Grace said, feeling wistful, more aware than ever that things were nothing like old times, and never would be again.

'So, you had an eventful first day, then.'

'Something like that.'

'Things will settle down once I put you to the grindstone. You'll be too tired for morning surfs on flat calm days for a start.'

'I've entered the beach gala surfing competition.'

Joan paused, a chip hanging out of her mouth like a drunken cigarette. 'Are you out of your mind?'

'I'm not expecting to win. Just to make a point.'

Joan laughed. 'You always were a stubborn one. Nothing's changed then.'

'I'll need a bit of practice, but it's like riding a bike, isn't it?'

Joan shrugged. 'You'd know.'

'Half the village is laughing at me now. On the day of the competition, they'll laugh no longer.'

'Depends on the weather,' Joan said. 'If we get some decent surf maybe, but if its flat calm like now they'll move the competition out to Sharker's Rock and no one will see it.'

'Except the guys laughing at me from the boat.'

'Ah, they're harmless. Developed a bit of a pride thing since you've been away, it looks like.'

'I have not.'

'Try sitting in one of these things for a while. You'll give it up pretty quick.'

'I'm sorry.'

Joan smiled. 'I'm only joking. You go for it. If I had my chance over ... well, never mind. Oh, here he comes.'

'Who?'

'Over there, see that white transit van? The Masked Surfer.'

Grace coughed, spitting bits of chip across the sand. A herring gull darted for a larger piece, claimed it with a muffled squawk, and retreated out of stone's throw range.

At the far southern end of the beach, where a stony road gave access to the foreshore and the surf club, an unmarked van had pulled up. A man, already wearing a wetsuit mask and sunglasses climbed out and walked further down the road until the rollers hitting Sharker's Rock came into view. He folded his arms and stood for a few minutes, watching.

'The Masked Surfer,' Joan said with an air of excitement. 'No one knows who he is, but he's a total badass.'

With a barely perceptible nod, the Masked Surfer returned to his van, opened the back doors and took out an old, battered surfboard. He stripped off his clothes to reveal a wetsuit underneath, then locked up the van and headed down the beach, surfboard under his arm.

'Who is he?'

'No one knows. He started showing up in the spring, parking up there—where you're not supposed to park— and hitting the surf. He comes down every few days, whenever the surf's up. I remember back in March we had a storm roll through, and he was the only one who went out. The sea was brutal, and he took it to pieces. Just aced it. Word got around, and by the time he came out there were thirty locals standing on the promenade in the pouring rain, just watching. Everyone reckons he's some professional trying to practice without getting attention, but you know, this is Cornwall. If he was a real pro he'd be off in Portugal or Hawaii or somewhere, wouldn't he?'

'Perhaps he's a local. Has anyone bothered to check the van's plates? That would tell you, wouldn't it?'

'Yeah, someone did. It's a rental from a firm in Truro. It changes from time to time too, and no one could get a real name.'

'Couldn't someone hire a private investigator?'

Joan laughed. 'Look at you, motivated city girl. This is Cornwall. We do things "dreckly" down here, as in when we get around to it. No rush, is there? And plus, if we hassle him too much he might go somewhere else. Look.'

Joan pointed up at the promenade. Several people had appeared, pints of beer, ice-creams, or bags of chips in hand, all watching the Masked Surfer as he paddled out towards Sharker's Rock, where a large swell was forming into majestic, clean rollers.

'He usually shows up just as the tide starts to turn,' Joan said. 'The swell out there isn't as powerful but the waves hold their shape better. There are a few shops which stay open late on high tide days just in case he shows, but the couple of times we tried it he didn't turn up. Mum likes to get back for *Eastenders*.'

Grace laughed, but she was only half listening. The Masked Surfer had reached the break now and was sitting in deep water, the swell lifting him up as it passed underneath. When a set began to form, he turned his board, waited for the biggest wave at the back, and paddled on to it.

Gasps and claps came from the promenade above. Grace stared as the Masked Surfer dropped into a big roller, disappeared for a moment, then reappeared again, riding the wave across the face. As it started to fade, he hacked the board upwards and executed a neat reverse jump, dropping back into the wave as it broke and riding it out, before dropping back onto his board and paddling back out.

'Woah.'

Joan laughed. 'Quite something, isn't he?'

'Takes some practice to do a move like that.'

They watched for a while as the Masked Surfer pulled off a series of epic turns and jumps. After about half an hour, with a wind beginning to blow in off the sea and the swells to flatten out, he rode one final wave before paddling back towards the beach.

Over by the van, a handful of people had gathered. A pair of local surfers patted him on the back as he opened up the van and loaded his gear, while a couple of girls appeared to offer their numbers, which the Masked Surfer waved away. Without removing his wetsuit or mask, he climbed into his van and backed off the top of the beach, turned, and headed away up Melrose Hill.

'Fantastic,' Grace said. 'He comes down here a lot?'

'Once a week or so,' Joan said.

'I wonder why he doesn't reveal his identity?'

'Would you?'

'If those guys were offering me their numbers, I probably would.'

'Unless you had a special reason,' Joan said. 'Perhaps he likes it. Perhaps the mystery excites him. It certainly excites the locals. Why ruin it by revealing that you're some nerd who works in a pasty factory or the dad of one of the local kids? Everyone loves a mystery, but the reveal is never as much fun as the thrill of wondering.'

'I guess you're right.'

With a sudden urgency, Joan began to shuffle back towards the chair. 'Time to go,' she said.

'Why?'

'It just is.'

'You need the toilet?'

'Shut up, nothing like that. It's just—'

Too late, Grace had seen him. Walking across the sand, holding a dog on a leash, was Daniel Woakes.

'Graceful, come on….'

'Wait.'

Joan had begun to sweat. Grace watched Daniel from a safe distance, warm memories coming back. He hadn't changed much. Filled out a little, maybe, but he was still the same Daniel she had almost—

'Dad! Wait!'

Joan was looking at the sand, but Grace couldn't take her eyes off Daniel as a little girl, no older than five or six, came running up behind him, grabbed him around the legs and leaned into a hug.

Grace looked at Joan. 'He has kids?' she said, throat dry.

Joan winced. 'Yeah, I meant to tell you about that.'

12

TEENAGE SUMMER

'GRACEFUL, YOU PROBABLY WANT TO EASE BACK A little bit.'

Grace finished what was left of her wine and immediately reached for the bottle to top herself up. 'It's a celebration, isn't it?' she said, aware her words were slurring. 'Our reunion. My return to Blue Sands. And … and … Daniel's happy marriage.'

As Joan's wavering face watched her with what Grace guessed were motherly eyes, she took a swig of her freshly filled glass and immediately coughed, getting a hand up just in time to stop the wine from spraying across the chalet's beige carpet.

'I bet she's a looker, isn't she? Like a fashion model. Or is she rich?'

Grace reached for the wine bottle, but Joan was quicker, pulling it out of Grace's reach, then lifting it and taking a swallow straight from the bottle itself.

'God, this stuff's rank,' she said, grimacing as she set the bottle back down. 'I know you're on a budget, but did you have to buy the cheapest one? I'd rather drink sea water.'

'I'm a failure,' Grace slurred.

'Daniel moved on, that's all. And yes, for what it's worth, she's very nice. Her name is Isabella. I think she's Spanish, but I've never asked.'

Grace slumped back in the armchair, sloshing a little wine over her blouse. She tried to wipe it up with a finger, but gave up, letting it soak in.

'I'm not disappointed, or sad, or desperate, or anything else. I'm happy for him. He's a good guy. He deserves to be happy. I just wish … I could be happy too.'

Joan rolled her eyes. 'Says you with the legs.'

'I didn't mean to be insensitive.'

'It's all right. The chair gives me a different perspective, that's all. You have to be in it, to see it, as you could say. Do you know what I see when I look at you?'

'A drunk?'

'Apart from that.'

'What?'

'Someone who's not quite sure where they're going in life. With Mum and Dad owning the café, I always had a safety net, and I realised I didn't mind it all that much, working there in the summer, even if we didn't make all that much money, because it was a nice life, getting to meet people, be around the beach, seeing kids smile when we overloaded the ice-creams or deliberately undercharged them for a bag of sweets. Winters have always kind of sucked, but it's not the end of the world. I found a place, and I'm happy. You were looking for more, but you haven't found it yet.'

'I thought I had, then it started to unravel.'

'Ah, Gavin was a tosspot. You're better off without him. And café jobs are ten a penny. You won't have to deal with any pretentious types working for me. Not many, anyway. They tend to go to Padstow.'

'What can I do?'

Joan leaned forward. Grace appreciated the gesture because for the last hour or more she'd been talking to a blur. Seeing her friend's face clearly again, she was able to appreciate the sincerity in Joan's words.

'I tell you what. We'll do it together. We're going to go old school, and have another teenage summer. Me and you, like we used to. Sure, I'm in the chair, and you're no longer able to hold your drink, but screw the fine print. We're going to live it up, have an awesome time, and when September rolls around and it starts to piss down every day, and all the tourists go home, we'll sit down together again, drink another bottle of wine, and figure out what you're going to do with your life. Until then, though, we're not going to worry about a thing. Deal?'

Grace felt a knot growing in her stomach. She felt like crying with love for Joan, but at the same time, she was beginning to feel a little uncomfortable.

'What is it, Grace?'

'I think I'm going to be sick.'

'Are you sure?'

Grace sat up. 'Yeah. Oh, god. The toilet's upstairs. Quick, open the screen door.'

'I can't. I'm a bloody invalid.'

Grace put her hands over her stomach. She managed to get up out of the chair and then was half running, half falling across the chalet's little living room. The screen door was closed, the lock one of those weird ones you had to twist two or three times and wait for the click. Grace was currently seeing three of them, which wouldn't help, so she looked around in desperation.

'The kitchen?'

'Where?'

'Over there.'

Grace shook her head. 'No time—'

Her hands closed over the only thing in range, a ceramic fruit bowl on a sideboard beside the screen doors. She held it close to her face, using her hair to block any backsplash.

'Wow, brutal.'

The eruption seemed to last an age. When finally her stomach stopped contracting, Grace opened her eyes to see a bowl of gunky red liquid. Holding it carefully, she carried it to the kitchen and poured it down the sink.

It took her a couple of minutes to wipe herself down to an acceptable standard. A glass of water helped to ease the ache in her stomach and the raw sensation at the back of her throat, and half a roll of kitchen towel got most of the bits out of her hair. When she returned to the living room, Joan gave a soft clap.

'That was magnificent. I can't believe you saved that.'

Grace groaned. 'Uh, thanks.'

'Perhaps best to leave off the wine for the rest of the night, or at least let me finish it. I can handle it a bit better than you by the look of things.'

Grace still felt queasy as she nodded. 'Sure.'

'So, do we have a deal, then? Are we going to live this summer like there's no tomorrow, with no worries, no regrets, and no silly baggage holding us back? Deal or no deal?'

Grace smiled. 'Deal.'

13

THE MOURNING LADY

Stage one of Joan's summer of excitement plan was a picnic out by Blue Point. As they headed up the cliff path, Grace straining as she pushed Joan's wheelchair, Joan gave her an ongoing pep talk.

'Look, I know it's more about taking part, but there's no harm in trying to win, is there? And if you can't even push me up this path you've got no chance of winning the bike race up Melrose Hill.'

'As long as I beat Jason King, I don't really care,' Grace said.

'At the moment you couldn't even beat me,' Joan answered. 'Come on, put your back into it. A little to the right here. There's a rut that'll catch the wheel if you stray too far to the left. They haven't quite cracked disabled access on the coast path yet.'

Even though Joan's wheelchair was one specially designed for outdoors with thick tires and an adjustable suspension, it was Joan herself who was more of a problem, having gained a fair amount of weight since becoming chair-bound. After lots of straining and groaning, they finally made it up to the flat part on top of the headland and Grace was happy to give her aching shoulders a rest as the headland sloped gently down towards Blue Point, on a promontory jutting out into the sea.

A little lighthouse stood at the end of the main headland, a quaint red cone, sadly now fully automated, operating only during select times of the year or in particularly bad weather. A gravel access road led away up the hill, passing through a farm gate and disappearing into the valley. Clustered around the lighthouse were a handful of picnic tables giving fine views of the coast to both north and south.

Past the lighthouse, the path led down from the headland's peak into a tiny, crescent-shaped cove. Cut off from the headland except for half an hour at low tide when a narrow, rocky channel became crossable by foot, Blue Point was a small rock stack which had somehow managed to escape the sea's onslaught. As teenagers, Grace and Joan had often climbed across to Blue Point despite their parents' warnings to be careful of the tide, which when high left only a metre of rock jutting above the water to be harassed endlessly by the waves. Now, though, they settled for the gravelly flat area just above the water line, on which someone had conveniently positioned a bench. Bleached by sea spray and half collapsed, it looked across the bay towards Sharker's Rock. From here, the beach and the village were hidden around the edge of the headland. In midsummer the spot was almost always occupied by groups of tourists, but today, in mid-June, they were alone.

'She hasn't changed,' Grace said, helping Joan down from the chair onto a blanket spread across the coarse couch grass behind the bench.

Joan looked up at the rock stack, which from this angle held a vague resemblance to a woman looking away from them at the sea, arms pulled tightly around her.

'She'll outlast all of us,' Joan said. 'She'll be waiting there for her lover to return for a thousand years after we're dead.'

The tale of the Mourning Lady of Blue Sands had captivated tourists for generations, since it had no doubt been invented by some local business owner for merchandising purposes, resulting in all manner of tacky goods which could be bought in the local shops. Even Joan's parents had given in to the sales revenue opportunity, stocking t-shirts, postcards, tea towels, history books, and even dramatic novelisations of the story, which had evolved over time.

The official story—in its current form at least—told of a woman called Lucy Pearce, the daughter of a local landowner. She had fallen in love with the son of a blacksmith, Peter Trevellian. Lucy had been betrothed to another, and her relationship with Peter kept secret. By night they had met here in this hidden spot, until the day Peter had been recruited to join the Napoleonic Wars. He had promised to return and marry Lucy, but according to the convoluted legend, he had died at sea, on the very day a larger sea stack had collapsed, leaving behind the shape of the Mourning Lady. Faced with marrying a man she didn't love, Lucy fled to the rock, and was drowned when the tide came in, and a particularly vicious storm struck the coast.

'An absolute load of rubbish,' Joan said, talking around a mouthful of tuna sandwich. 'No more truth in it than all that stuff about King Arthur further up the coast.'

Grace smiled. 'How many Mourning Lady postcards did you sell last week?'

Joan rolled her eyes. 'Mum wants to start stocking the CD.'

'The CD?'

'Oh man, you've been away too long. You must have missed that. A local pub band called We Are Cornish Folk brought out a song called The Ballad of Lucy Pearce. It was a massive hit on Radio Cornwall, and apparently on Spotify—for a week at least—it outranked BTS in the Southwest.'

'Like when Rootjoose took on the Spice Girls?'

'Yeah, Mum always goes on about that.'

'I wonder what happened to them?'

Joan shrugged. 'One of them came in for an ice-cream last week. Not sure which one. Can't recognise them with short hair, and he's filled out a bit.'

'Better to be famous for five minutes than never at all.'

'And you're going to be famous for winning the Melrose Hill Bicycle Race. And you're going to do it faster than walking pace.'

'Fingers crossed.' Grace smiled. 'You know, I know it's kind of ridiculous, but I was thinking about what you said about reliving our youth and all that, and I've decided to do it on the BMX.'

Joan coughed out a mouthful of sandwich. 'Please tell me you're not serious. I just kept that bike for a laugh. I didn't expect you to actually ride it. And certainly not up Melrose Hill.'

'It only has three gears, and I haven't grown much since I was fourteen.'

'You'll be a laughing stock.'

'I think that's inevitable. Don't worry, it'll be fun.'

Joan's smile dropped, and her voice took on a somber tone. 'Grace. Spotlight will be there. It'll be televised.'

'Seriously?'

'They showed up last year. It chucked it down with rain and the race got abandoned, but I think they were interested enough to come back.'

Grace shrugged and grinned. 'Better to be famous for five minutes.'

They ate in silence for a while. Grace looked out across the bay towards Sharker's Rock, where a handful of surfers were riding gentle sets bending around the headland. In the cove itself, the water was a flat calm mirror. Several people were swimming far enough out that she could see them, even though the beach itself was out of sight.

'I've missed this place,' she said. 'I can see why you stay.'

'Ah, but when you're stuck here through the winter you can see why so many people leave.'

'Hasn't your mum got a year-round license yet?'

Joan shook her head. 'She hasn't greased enough palms at the county council. Sophie at the Gourmet Garden got one a couple of years ago, but the rumour was that she had to bang a couple of councillors to get it. Locals started calling it the Shag Shack.'

'But she's what, fifty?'

'And the rest. Most of the councillors are dinosaurs, though. I imagine it's a load of rubbish, but you know what people are like round here. After I came out of hospital in the chair, I told a couple of people I'd been shot, and a week or so later one of the old dears at the bowls club asked Mum if the police had caught the shooter yet.'

Grace laughed, almost dropping a flask of coffee. 'The good and bad of small towns,' she said. 'Everyone's willing to help you out, but at the same time your entire life is common knowledge.'

Joan smiled. 'I wouldn't have it any other way. By the way, you start work tomorrow. Are you ready?'

'I've waited a million tables. Easy.'

'I know you can do the job. I'm not talking about that. Daniel Woakes comes in every morning for a newspaper. Can you handle that?'

14

OLD FLAME

THE LAYOUT OF THE BLUE SANDS CAFÉ AND SHOP HAD changed a little since Grace had last been inside. The shop area was still to the right, with the café to the left, but where before customers could only access one at a time by separate outside doors, the former partition wall had now been knocked through so customers could move back and forth. The shop area looked a little smaller to Grace before she realised the counter had been moved forward to accommodate Joan's wheelchair, but otherwise it looked the same as ever. The same racks of books and postcards, boxes of buckets and spades, trinkets made out of shells, local art prints in stacks, some rusty ship parts found on the beach still hanging from the ceiling. The same tea towels hung from the walls, the same chocolate bars filled the rack on the counter, and barring the addition of honeycomb, the ice-cream flavours hadn't changed.

'That can of dandelion and burdock we could never sell is still there,' Joan said, pointing at the soft drinks fridge. 'Although it's now nineteen years out of date so we're not officially allowed to sell it. Mum put a vintage sticker on it as a kind of joke, just in case one of those council inspectors comes round.'

The cakes counter, with its Eccles cakes, cheesecakes, and caramel shortbread, looked identical. The pasty selection had expanded to include pork and apple on top of the usual steak and cheese and onion varieties.

'Mum wanted to order in chicken tikka ones,' Joan said, tapping the glass of the heated oven display. 'Partly to reflect the changing times, and partly because they're lush. Dad put his foot down, though. Called it a sacrilege. Won't touch the pork ones, even though they're lush, too.'

Grace hooked an apron over her head and tied the strings around her waist. 'Ready for business,' she said. 'I think.'

'You can hide in the back room if you want,' Joan said. 'He usually comes in around nine. I'll call you when he's gone.'

Grace shook her head. 'It's not like I'm setting myself up to rekindle our relationship,' she said. 'He's married. He has kids. I just need to get this over with as quickly as possible, so it's not going to be awkward between us for the rest of the summer.'

'Try not to say or do anything stupid,' Joan said. 'His wife and kids often come in for ice-creams. And don't tell Mum I told you, but we need the business. There's a lot of competition around these days, and with the Gourmet Garden getting its year-round license, it gets all the loyalty from locals.'

'I'll try not to,' Grace said. 'But yeah, if you see his wife and kids, I really would like to hide in the back for that one.'

'Noted.' Joan clapped her hands together. 'Right. Let's get ready for opening. For obvious reasons, you can put all the beach gear racks outside while I stock up the pasties.'

They got to work. As she carried racks of buckets and spades, postcards, and polystyrene surfboards outside, a light, chilly breeze ruffling her hair, Grace felt a moment of almost pure peace. It really hadn't changed all that much from when she was a teenager. The beach still looked the same, the sounds of the sea and the birds felt like old friends, and the breeze tugging on the polystyrene surfboard she carried felt almost playful.

'Are you open yet?' came a gruff man's voice from behind her. Grace turned, and found herself faced with a rugged man in shorts, a check shirt and hiking boots, with a heavy rucksack on his back.

Grace checked her watch. 'About five minutes, but you can go inside, the pasty counter might be ready.'

The man smiled. 'How did you know?'

'Coast path walkers are always the first customers of the day,' she said. 'Which way are you heading?'

'North. Aiming for Newquay today.'

'Wow, that's quite a distance.'

The man turned his face up to the clear sky. 'Looks a good day for it. Figured I'd press on while I could. Rain due in a day or two.'

'Good idea. Go on in.'

The man smiled thanks and went inside. As a teenager, Grace had never seen the appeal in slogging around the undulating Southwest Coast Path, with its total change of elevation equal to climbing Everest four times, but now she was older, and much of a fitness freak, she could understand. All those hours with only the cliffs, the sea, and the sky for company, especially in the modern world when your mind was forever cluttered with due dates, appointments, and social media interactions. It was idyllic.

Grace continued to arrange the racks around the front of the shop. A couple of minutes later, the hiker reappeared with a couple of wrapped pasties under his arm.

'Thank you kindly,' he said.

'Have a good day.'

'Will do.'

Grace watched him walk across the road and along the promenade. At the corner he turned out of sight. If she walked out a little way, she could see the coastal path rising up to the headland, so she wondered if she would see him in a few minutes, climbing slowly up. It made her think of journeys, in particular her own. A few days ago she had felt like she had stalled somewhat, but now it was more of a pit stop, a chance for refueling and repair before continuing on. Who knew what the future held? By this time next year, she could be a—

'Excuse me, have the papers arrived yet?'

Grace froze. Almost too afraid to turn around, she replayed the words in her mind, recalling the soft but powerful intonation, the firmness in the words that she had once found so electric. He was standing there, right behind her, his shadow stretching over hers as though they were entwined once again, all these years after she had let him go.

'I think so,' she said, her voice little more than a dry-throated croak. 'Why don't you go inside?'

The shadow didn't move. Grace felt a cold sweat breaking out across her back. She clutched the polystyrene surfboard hard enough to crease its spongy surface.

'Grace … is that you?'

She turned, and there he stood behind her, lit by the morning sun above the hills, a glow given to a face that was a fine vintage version of the one she had adored as a teenager, all handsome angles and gentle curves. She wasn't sure what she had expected now that she was seeing him in closeup; after all, they were the same age, but Daniel looked as good, if not better than he had during their few months together ten years ago. He was wider at the shoulders, a little more rugged with a hint of stubble, his hair a fraction longer, but the deep brown of his eyes was the same, the arch of his nose, the smile when it came—

'Yes, it's me.'

She turned away before she could do or say something stupid, making a show of putting the last polystyrene surfboard into the rack outside the door.

'I heard you were back.'

So, the cat was out, the beans spilled. Grace steeled herself, looked up, and nodded.

'Just for the summer.'

'It's great to see you. Really, I mean it.'

Grace forced a smile. It wasn't great to see him. It reminded her of what she had walked away from, what she had lost. She could be standing in a mirror position to now, beside him, holding his hand perhaps. The little girl she had seen could be theirs. She could be running the Low Anchor by his side, walking on the beach on summer mornings, lying beside him at night.

Instead she was eking out an existence in a café in Bristol, being hit on and insulted by rich idiots, pretending that she was on the road to making it, whatever that meant, when the man she had left in order to pursue her dream of undefined success had done everything she had not in her absence.

'It's not great to see you,' she muttered, thinking it was a whisper too low to be heard, but realising the wind had dropped at exactly the wrong moment, giving her words a quiet, distant songbird clarity that made Daniel frown.

'Oh, right. Well—'

'I didn't mean it!' she snapped quickly, reaching out and grabbing his arm before she could get control over what she was doing. She felt thick muscle beneath his shirt; the surfer's beef had gone hard from hauling beer barrels. She couldn't imagine what he looked like without the shirt, but she doubted it would be a disappointment.

He had a small smile on his face. 'You're pinching me.'

Grace let go. 'Oh. I'm sorry. This is a bit awkward. Look, I'm happy to see you, Daniel. Just, you know, it's weird.'

He smiled again, and she felt her heart melting just like it had ten years before. Only this time, rather than warm and sticky like a Danish pastry, it felt weak and flat like ice-cream left in the sun. His arms belonged around someone else now; she had given them up and had to live with it.

'I hope we can hang out sometime. I'd like to introduce you to Isabella. She's always interested in meeting my old friends.'

Grace stared at him, throat dry. 'Friends?'

Daniel's smile turned cheeky, the way it always had when he was about to suggest something a little risqué, like a midnight tryst out at Blue Point or a drive up the cliff in his battered old VW Beetle to watch the sunrise, something that had never involved just watching.

'Well, I'd have to tell her that, wouldn't I? I don't think she'd appreciate the full details. She's not the jealous type, but you know … you've aged well, Grace.'

'What's that supposed to mean?'

He gave a suggestive shrug. 'You've hardly aged. You look great.'

Grace felt her cheeks turn tomato red. She felt the sweat beading under her brow, and she hoped the sun was bright enough that he couldn't see it.

'You look good too,' she said, immediately regretting

her words, feeling as though she was hitting on him. 'I mean, you've not got fat or bald, and you still have both eyes.'

'For the time being. The birds get a little close sometimes, but they've not been quite hungry enough. How long are you staying? Did you move back down?'

'Just for a few months.'

'Things not working out up there? Where is it, Bristol?'

'I just felt like a change of scenery.'

Daniel nodded. 'Well, there's no better place. Summers have been a lot nicer recently. Global warming and all that.'

'That's good. Uh, I mean about the weather.'

Their conversation having shifted to something as shockingly mundane as discussing the weather, Grace began to feel a little more comfortable, although she was already missing the almost flirtatious thrill of their opening salvo.

Daniel glanced over his shoulder, as though someone was waiting for him. 'Well, I'd better get back. Got to get the kids' breakfast.'

'Aren't they late for school?'

'It's Saturday.'

'Ah, right.'

'It was nice to see you again, Grace. Maybe we'll see each other about?'

It was framed as a question, so Grace gave a nod as he stepped past her, heading into the shop. She looked at his back, the broad shoulders, the powerful hips she'd once had license to hold, and realised she couldn't face him again on the way out. She turned and fled down the alley beside the shop, around to the back, where she used a key Joan had given her to go in through the back door, into a room crammed with stock. A small staff toilet cubicle stood to the side, so Grace slipped inside and locked the door.

She had been sitting there for a few minutes when a gentle knock came on the door.

'Grace? Are you still alive in there?'

Not sure what she would say to anyone, Grace unlocked the door and pushed it open. Joan sat there in her chair, a motherly smile on her face.

'I'm guessing you met Daniel? Don't worry, he's gone now.'

Grace started to get up, but found she couldn't move. 'It was awful,' she said, feeling tears run down her cheeks. 'I thought I could handle it, but I couldn't.'

Then, sobbing like a child, she leaned forward and laid her head on Joan's lap.

'There, there,' Joan said, patting her on the back as she cried. 'You'll be fine. I really wish this could have happened somewhere other than the toilet, though.'

15

PRIVATE AUDIENCE

She hadn't expected to pull it off on the first attempt, but as she leaned forward on the bike, lungs bursting, then looked back around at the pathetic distance she'd made it up Melrose Hill before her strength gave out, she knew she had a long way to go if she was even going to compete in the race without embarrassing herself.

From here, just beyond the bulge of the Singing Rock, she wasn't even high enough to see the beach. The toughest stretch was still above her, with the bulge doing its business like it always had, the switchback so sharp that any momentum built in the run up was stolen away, meaning you had to take on the longer section almost from a standing start. Frustrated, she climbed back onto the pink BMX, pedaled a couple of futile metres, then decided it was time for breakfast.

She was just turning back downhill when an older woman wearing shorts and a t-shirt appeared around the bend, leading an unkempt but jovial golden retriever on a thick leash.

Grace stared. As the woman reached her, she couldn't help but say, 'Mrs. Oldfield? Is that you?'

The woman looked up. She frowned for a couple of seconds before recognition spread across her face. 'Grace Clelland? Well, I'll never. I thought you were long gone. Down for a holiday?'

Grace smiled. 'Something like that. You look well.'

The woman who had been Grace's secondary school art teacher scowled. 'I can still do the dragon if the kids are kicking their balls a little too close to my drive,' she said. 'Alas, sometimes I wish they would. These days they just stand around staring at those silly devices in their hands. The art of conversation has died.'

'It's the modern world, isn't it?'

'I'm glad to see that you're at least getting out and about. You're not really trying to cycle up Melrose on this old thing, are you?'

Grace laughed and patted the bike. 'I'm reliving my youth.'

Mrs. Oldfield lifted an eyebrow. 'Rather you than me. I think I'd empty the streets if I did the same. Especially in those lycra shorts. Kids have gone soft since the switch got outlawed.'

The dog nosed at Grace's feet. She reached down to give the thick fur coat a stroke. 'This isn't really Trixie, is it? I mean, she looks just like her.'

Mrs. Oldfield laughed. 'No, this is Daisy, Trixie's granddaughter. She's just five years old. I've still got Trixie's daughter, Penny, at home, but she's twelve now and can't handle the hill. I just walk her around the village in the evening. Poor old Trixie, she lived to nearly seventeen. Had a good life, that old dog.'

'It's been lovely to meet you again, Mrs. Oldfield,' Grace said.

'And you, dear. Are you staying locally?'

'Down in one of the chalets. Actually, I'll be working in the café with Joan over the summer.'

'Oh, how lovely. Like when you were teenagers, skipping out of school to surf instead of handing in your homework.'

Grace felt an old shudder of fear as Mrs. Oldfield's tone turned dark. Just as she was about to apologise for whatever assignment she had lied about completing, Mrs. Oldfield laughed.

'Ha, look at you, dear. Having kittens. Once a teacher, always a teacher. You have a lovely day.'

'Thanks, and you.'

Grace watched Mrs. Oldfield and Daisy make their way slowly up Melrose Hill, the dog taking the lead while the old lady made switchbacks to make the climb easier. Mrs. Oldfield appeared in no hurry, regularly pausing by the hedgerow to gaze into the fields and across the valley at the beach. She decided to take a leaf out of the old teacher's book, perhaps try to calm down, be a little less hard on herself. In the city she had felt caught in an ongoing stampede towards success, one that she had found herself near the back of, struggling to keep up. But what was she really looking for?

She free-wheeled back down the hill to the chalet, took a shower, and got ready for work. It was a pleasant day, warm, a few clouds in the air, a light breeze blowing off the sea. The school holidays and the influx of tourists were still some weeks away, but Blue Sands was starting to fill with retired couples and small groups taking advantage of the weather before the kids took over. By mid-morning, the café was full, with a handful of other retired types in the shop, browsing the books and postcards.

'You're my lucky charm,' Joan said, wheeling up beside

Grace, who stood in the shop behind the pasty counter. 'Business has been great since you came back.'

'Wasn't it before?'

Joan grimaced. 'Truth be told, last summer sucked. It rained all the time, and we had a hard time keeping up with her up the road and her specials menu. Apparently Sophie did a cooking course last winter, and all her sautéed steaks and bologna sausage stews kept us locked out of the main food crowd. Food is where the money is. We have to sell a hundred postcards to make a penny.'

'I didn't know.'

Joan looked about to say something else, but then gave a small smile and turned back to the café counter where a young couple were waiting to order.

'Hi guys, how can I help you?'

That night, Joan said she had some accounting to do, so sent Grace home, an unsold pasty wrapped and under her arm for tea. Rather than go back to the chalet, though, Grace decided to walk up the southern cliff path, out towards Sharker's Rock. With the sun low in the sky, the breeze had got up, so she wrapped a light wind cheater around her shoulders and tucked the pasty inside. The path was a gentle undulation through mounds of couch grass and past blankets of impenetrable gorse and heather. The view of Blue Sands Cove opened out below her as she climbed, the path extending for a mile or so along rolling cliffs until you reached a final inaccessible lump, below which was the remote headland of Sharker's Rock.

At the best viewing spot of the bay to the north, the council had erected a bench, dedicated to a deceased local called William Benn who had regularly walked his dog to this spot. As Grace sat down on what the locals now called William bench, she noticed a shape moving through the water.

The Masked Surfer.

From here, she wouldn't have been able to recognise his identity even without his mask, but in full surfing gear she had no chance. She let her imagination run wild, wondering if he was perhaps some locally-living TV celebrity, practicing his art in anonymity. This evening the break was pretty low over the reef of slate outcrops around Sharker's Rock, but as Grace slowly ate her pasty, she watched him make the most of it, cutting and weaving through the curling tubes with obvious mastery, catching the waves at the exact moment that they peaked, riding the glassy faces perfectly as the tubes crashed onto the jagged slate just a couple of feet below the surface.

You had to be good to surf the reef by Sharker's Rock. Grace had done it a couple of times, but it was not for the faint-hearted, and she'd rarely felt daring enough. With the underwater rocks causing the break, a mistake could prove costly. She was lucky enough that she didn't know anyone who had drowned, but a couple of guys her age had got hammered in a fall and limped back to shore with broken bones.

The Masked Surfer, however, had a pro look about him. He seemed to know precisely which waves were right and which were just too steep or breaking just too close to the rocks, pulling out of a couple of rides that looked safe to Grace. She watched him with wonder, feeling special, that she was privy to a private session, something few others saw.

The sun was just touching the horizon when the Masked Surfer decided his work for the evening was done. He took one last wave, riding it to the end this time rather than cutting out. As the wave died, he lowered himself back to the board and began paddling for the distant beach.

Grace stood up without really thinking about what she was doing. She had long ago finished her pasty, so she stuffed the paper wrapper into her pocket, patted William bench goodbye, and started walking back along the cliff path.

Even though the Masked Surfer had to paddle all the way across the bay and then walk up to the foreshore from the low tide mark, Grace would have to hurry to catch him. Walking quickly on the upward slopes and jogging lightly on the down, she reached the bottom of the path just as the Masked Surfer was walking across the shingle of the foreshore, his wetsuit glistening as the sun set behind him.

His van was parked on the beach access road as before. Grace slowed her pace in order to reach it just as he stood his board up against the side, took a key out of a pocket inside the neck of his wetsuit and opened the back door.

She could smell the salt water on him, mixed with the smells of wax from his board and the rubber of his suit. He had his back to her, and she quickly sized him up: he was a shade over six feet, powerfully built, his shoulders broad. She wondered how hard they would feel to the touch.

Barely an arms' length away she stopped. *Speak*, she compelled herself, trying to channel Joan's inner strength long enough to flap her own natural shyness away.

'Nice rides,' she said, a little phlegm catching in her throat at exactly the wrong time to make the words sound like the receding tide drawing sand back through shingle.

He looked back as though he had known she was there, and Grace found herself regarding a pair of sky blue eyes, the only part of his face that was visible besides the tip of his nose and a line for his mouth.

'Thanks,' he said, his voice deeper than she had expected, as though he was intentionally making it so.

'Are you local? I can tell you know the reef out at Sharker's Rock well.'

His shoulder twitched in what might have been a shrug. 'Local enough,' he said. Then, to avoid any further comment, he leaned down to pull the Velcro leash strap off his ankle. Grace found herself staring at the lower flap of his wetsuit mask. While you couldn't have pulled it off from gripping the front, by putting your fingers under the flap you could peel it off his head, and if he tried to pull away it would only speed up the process.

Her hand twitched, but she pulled it back at the last moment.

She preferred the mystery.

A moment later, he stood up again, and the chance was gone.

'I used to surf out there,' she said. 'Going back a few years. I've been out of the game a while.'

He watched her, unspeaking. Gave a small nod.

'I mean, I'd love to try it again, but I'm a little nervous.'

'Guys go out at high tide, I hear,' he said. 'You're safe among others.'

'But no one tries it at low tide, when the waves are really steep. No one except you.'

He gave another little shrug. 'So?'

'Aren't you scared?'

He watched her, a smile under the mask. 'No.'

'Maybe you could take me out sometime,' she said, her heart thundering so loud she thought she might cough or even vomit up her pasty. 'I'd love to learn from … a master.'

He cocked his head a little. 'You're the shorebreak girl.'

Grace took a step back, out from the shadow behind his van into the glare of the setting sun, hoping it would hide the red flush in her cheeks.

'My name's Grace,' she said.

She sensed another smile. 'I know,' he said. 'Nice to meet you, Grace.' Then, closing the door of his van, he added, 'I'd better get going.'

'Do you have a name?' she said, trailing after him as he went around to the driver's side.

He glanced back. 'I do.' That hidden smile again. 'See you around, Grace.'

He climbed up into the van, sitting on a towel Grace saw was already draped over the seat. He closed the door, then gave her a little wave as he started up the engine and backed up the beach access, out onto the main road. Another wave, then he was turning the van around, and driving up Melrose Hill, the rumble of the engine slowly receding into the distance.

16

BARBEQUE TRUTHS

'I NEED TO FIND OUT WHO HE IS,' GRACE SAID, TURNING a sausage over on the barbeque she had set up on the small patch of grass at the front of the chalet. 'I can't stop thinking about him.'

Joan shook her head. 'Do you think that'll stop you thinking about Daniel?'

'It might.'

'You know, Grace, I know you'd love this to be some kind of cool movie-type thing, but you're going to be disappointed. I just know it. He'll be like some weirdo or something. Why would he bother with the mask otherwise?'

'Because he likes being mysterious?'

'Look, the only people who wear masks do it for a reason. Either they're hiding something, or they're rough. Think, Jason Vorhees, the Phantom of the Opera.'

'One's a kind of zombie and the other's a disfigured opera singer. This guy's just a surfer. Perhaps he's trying to stay warm?'

'Then why not take off the mask when he's back on the

beach? He's been coming here for several months and no one's ever seen his face. He could be a serial killer on the run.'

'I doubt it.'

'Did you get a look in the back of his van? Were there any meat hooks?'

Grace smiled and shook her head. 'Not that I could see. It was empty.'

'I imagine he just takes his victims back to some processing factory.'

'I think you're overreacting.'

Joan took a sip from a glass of wine. 'We'll see.'

'Hey,' Grace said, nodding towards the road that passed the line of chalets, heading up the valley. 'There's Jason King. Let's see what he knows. Jason!'

The young owner of J's Surf Shack stopped at the gate. He had a rucksack slung over one shoulder and looked like he'd just finished work.

'You all right there?' Jason asked.

'Are you on your way home?'

Jason shrugged. 'Yeah, just finished clearing up. That barbeque looks hot.'

'It is. You got time for a chat?'

Jason gave an awkward shrug which reminded Grace of the library nerd he had once been, unsure whether he had been invited to the party or not.

'I've got burgers that are cooked and buns that are toasted if you tell me what you know about the Masked Surfer.'

'Who?'

'The guy with the transit van who surfs the reef off Sharker's Rock.'

Jason came in through the gate and threw his rucksack down on the grass. 'You mean Billy?'

'Billy? Is that his name?'

Jason shrugged. 'I don't know. Just what I call him. Not gonna call him "the Masked Surfer" or anything silly like that.'

'And Billy is a better name?'

Jason shrugged. 'Sure.'

'Do you know anything about him?' Joan asked, handing Jason a can of beer from a cooler.

'Wow, look at this, cold beer too,' Jason said, staring at the can of Carlsberg as though he'd never seen a beer before.

Grace smiled and lifted the glass of wine she was holding. 'Welcome to the party, Jason. Cheers, everyone.'

Jason popped his can and lifted it up with the same awkward reluctance he did everything else, it seemed. 'Happy summer time,' he said, flashing a bashful smile.

'And the waves rose high and the kraken smiled,
For dinner he could see, could see,
The sailors wailed as the ship topped and tailed,
And sank into the sea so green, so green!'

Grace and Joan laughed as Jason, arms spread, brought his drunken sea shanty to an end, nudging the foldout table with his knee to produce a rattle of cutlery.

'Where on earth did you learn that?' Joan asked.

'Tiktok,' Jason said, sipping his beer.

Grace rolled her eyes. 'You mean Facebook for twelve-year-olds.'

'And they upload sea shanties?' Joan asked.

Jason grinned. 'Apparently it's a thing. I'll learn a couple more for next time.'

'Next time?'

He shrugged. 'You're going to make this a regular thing, right?'

'This what?'

'This party.'

Grace looked around, eyes a little blurry even though she'd been more responsible after nearly repainting the chalet's living room the other day. There was only Joan, sitting in her chair, and Jason from J's Surf Shack, but he was right. They'd had a ball, drinking, eating, telling jokes, singing ridiculous songs. It was just what she had needed.

'It's summer,' she said. 'Why on earth not?'

'That's great,' Jason said. 'Blue Sands has gone a little flat the last couple of years. We need to liven it up a little.' He glanced at his watch. 'Anyway, I'd better go. Work in the morning.'

'Same,' Joan slurred. 'Night, Jason.'

He waved them farewell then headed down the path and up the road out of sight. Grace began to tidy up, but Joan put up a hand.

'Leave that,' she said, then added with a smirk, 'You can do it in the morning. I'll let you come in an hour late.'

'Thanks.'

Joan was already pushing her chair towards the chalet doors. 'Come on,' she said. 'I have something I need to tell you.'

'What?'

'It's freezing out here. Let's get inside first.'

Grace doused the last embers of the barbeque, which they had kept going to warm them as the chill evening winds whistled up the valley with increasing frequency, then helped Joan get her chair inside. Closing the doors on the night, she helped Joan onto the sofa, then went to the kitchen and made two coffees.

'Look at us,' Joan said, taking her coffee from Grace and resting it on her lap. 'A couple of old maids. Wasn't so long ago our last nightcap would have been a Sambuca slammer and a final desperate turn of the dancefloor.'

'We're not done yet,' Grace said, then let out a ridiculous belch which had her grasping for her mouth as though to catch the offending monstrosity before it escaped too far. 'Well, not quite done.'

Joan was staring at the coffee in her hands. 'Mum and Dad are selling up,' she said.

'What?'

'The house, the café, everything.'

'You're having a laugh.'

'I wish. Dad got offered a promotion to his company's head office in Plymouth. He's pretty old so it's his last chance, really. Means they're going to move up Dartmoor way rather than have him commute from down here. Mum could have kept the café, but really, it's been her pet for years. Dad's job's been propping it up.'

'What about you?'

'What about me?'

'Can't you run it?'

Leaving the coffee dangerously perched in her midriff, Joan spread her arms. 'Look at me. Do you really think I'm capable of it?'

'I know the chair makes things difficult. You could get staff in—'

'We survive at the moment because Mum and me pay ourselves starvation wages. We're not exactly making you rich either, are we?'

'But you can't just sell up. It's been in your family for years.'

'And it needs fresh blood. Someone with energy. Mobility. New ideas.'

'What if you applied for the year-round license? Would that make a difference?'

'We'd never get it. One of us would have to sleep with old Tomlinson, the councillor in charge of planning permission.'

'How old is he? Or more to the point, how young is he?'

Joan laughed. 'At least eight-five. Probably more. He looks it at any rate.'

'Well, I guess that's out of the question. Knowing my luck, he'd probably turn me down anyway.'

'I appreciate your willingness to take one for the team. However, I think old Tomlinson would prefer his palms greased in a different way. And we're barely making enough of that to keep the lights on.'

'Then we have to think of something else.'

Joan was staring at Grace, who realised she was leaning forward in the chair, the coffee clutched earnestly between her fingers.

'I don't think you heard me, did you? The café's being sold. It's not open for debate. Mum and Dad are tacking it on to the house sale in order to make the deal more attractive, and when they move, I'll probably have to go with them. You're acting like we could keep the café open if we make it successful enough. It's not going to happen. If you think it is, you must be drunker than me.'

Maybe it was the drink, maybe not, but as Grace stared at Joan, concentrating to stop her eyesight from blurring, she saw something there that Joan's words tried to hide: hope.

17

RIVAL

'I WISH I'D NEVER SAID ANYTHING.'

A few days later, and Joan was still grumbling about her drunken confession. 'It's put a cloud over everything. Mum's not going to put the sign outside until the end of the season anyway, so I wasn't going to tell you at all.'

'I'm glad you did. It gives me time to do something about it.'

'There's nothing you can do.'

Grace stopped polishing the pasty oven and turned to Joan, who was on the other side of the counter, replenishing the display of chocolate bars.

'Look. I have big city experience. I have ideas.'

'Like what?'

Grace shook her head. 'I don't know, like—'

'Exactly. You don't know.' The rumble of a van came from outside, making Joan turn. 'Hold that thought. The pasties are here.'

A van with a pasty company logo pulled up outside. Through the windows, a man in a blue and black uniform got out, went around the back, and unloaded several boxes on to a trolley, which he then wheeled through the door, hoicking it open expertly with one foot before reversing the trolley inside.

'Got your frozen,' he said, righting the trolley and sliding the stack of boxes off into a neat pile. 'Just get your fresh.'

Grace stared at the man's departing back, then turned to Joan. 'Was that Hedges?' she asked, unable to keep the incredulity out of her voice. 'I mean, the sideburns are a giveaway, but—'

'He won six figures on the lottery,' Joan said, giving a little shake of her head. 'And of all the things to buy, you'd never have guessed he'd buy a pasty company.'

'I've never heard of Suncrust Pasties,' Grace said.

'It used to be Dirgil's, that god awful packet supermarket brand that we used to rip on. Remember that chant whenever some kid had one in their lunchbox?'

Grace smiled. 'Dirgil's, Dirgil's, fit for gerbils.'

'That was it. I think there were verses but I can't remember them now. They went bankrupt. Hedges bought up what was left and turned it into Suncrust.'

The door opened. Hedges, sideburns pressing out from beneath his Suncrust Pasties cap, smiled. 'Feel like me ears are burning,' he said.

Joan nodded at Grace. 'Do you remember Grace Clelland, Steve?'

Steve Hedge set down the trolley and frowned. 'Grace … yeah, I remember. You guys were chums, right?'

Grace winced. It was Hedges, without a doubt. The weird kid from a couple of years below them at school, who used to spend his lunchtimes kicking a squashed Coke can around a corner of the playground because no one would let him join their games. As someone a couple of years older and several degrees cooler, Grace had barely registered him on her periphery, noticeable only for the sideburns which he had sported from as soon as he was old enough to grow them. No one had ever seemed to know him personally, and on the couple of times she had thought of him since leaving school, she had found it most likely he would end up in a boring corner desk position in a local council or insurance office.

No longer the spotty outcast, he had grown tall, his shoulders filled out, no doubt from lugging boxes of pasties about on a daily basis. And, dare she even think it, while certainly no standout, there was an angle about him that was almost handsome.

'It looks like you've done well for yourself, Hed—I mean, Steve.'

Hedges shrugged. 'Suppose so.' He gave a nervous scratch of his right sideburn, a relic from the nineteen sixties. 'Done okay.'

There was an awkward moment as they faced each other in a triangle before Hedges tipped his cap and bid them goodbye. Grace watched as the van pulled away.

'He supplies half the cafés for twenty miles in each direction,' Joan said. 'He also has three local bakeries. He's turned Dirgil's from a laughing stock into a proper contender. And he married Motormouth.'

'Becky Rendle?'

'The one and only. She's Becky Hedge now, believe it or not.'

'No....'

'These are strange days, Graceful. That's life for you.'

Grace stared out of the window after the departed pasty van. 'That's it,' she said. 'That's how we can stop your mum selling the café.'

Joan rolled her eyes. 'Employ Becky Hedge? Tried it last summer. She scared the customers away.'

'No, I don't mean that. Didn't you see the side of his van? The logo. *Suncrust Pasties – the taste of crispy.*'

'Yeah, it's ridiculous.'

'I know it is, but at the same time it's perfect. Do you remember the number one thing we used to complain about? How soggy those Dirgil's pasties were. Lumps of soft, cold pasty with soft, cold meat inside. He's taken the very thing that no one liked about them and used the exact opposite as his calling card.'

'And how is that supposed to save the café?'

Grace clapped her hands together. 'You need something similar. A logo. A catchphrase. Something universal but unique at the same time.'

'Like what?'

Grace opened her mouth to speak, but for once, nothing would come out.

'I'll think of something,' she said.

'Day off?' Jason asked as Grace came through the door. 'Thanks for the barbeque the other night. It was great.'

'You'll be a legend with those sea shanties,' Grace said. 'Are you free this Saturday night? I agree with what you said. Let's make these barbeques a regular thing.' Even as she said it, she realised what a warm feeling the idea gave her. 'I'll invite a few extra people each week, until it becomes the go-to party for the summer.'

Jason smiled. 'You're ambitious, I'll give you that. After a rental today?'

'Actually, I was wondering who made your shop's logo. You've got those cool t-shirts over there by the door. I just wondered who designed it. Was it some online company?'

Jason fiddled with his fingers, his cheeks flushing red.

'Ah, yeah. That.'

'Do you have an email address or a website?'

'Mrs. Oldfield.'

Grace stared. 'Excuse me? As in, the teacher Mrs. Oldfield? With the golden retrievers?'

'Ah, yeah. Used to be an art teacher, didn't she?'

'So she did.'

'She's friends with my mum. They're part of the same wickerwork club. Meet first Tuesday of the month. Mum told her I'd bought the shop, and the next month Mum comes home with this logo drawn on a piece of paper. And it was bang on the money.'

'That's great.'

'Yeah, we sell loads. Mostly to tourists. They love a good souvenir. Locals won't be seen dead wearing anything with my name on it.' His cheeks were still red, but he was looking at her now with an earnestness that made her uncomfortable. 'Listen, could I ask you something?'

No. He wasn't about to ask her out, surely? Grace felt a tremble of fear. He was a lovely guy, but not her type at all. He was too short for a start, not that she wanted to discriminate. No doubt he looked good in a wetsuit, but he just had a goofiness to him that she couldn't unsee.

'Sorry, I've got to get back to the café. I'm on lunch.'

He shrugged. 'Sure, no worries.'

Grace backed out, information gleaned but also a possible proposition strung out with fairy lights between them. What was she going to do? She had already invited him to the barbeque. Still, it was a few days away. She could plan a suitable response in the meantime, one that wouldn't let him down too harshly, one that would allow them to remain friends.

Outside, she was about to head back towards the café when a voice made her heart sink.

'Grace! Over here!'

She looked up. Daniel stood across the street on the promenade, but he wasn't alone. A tall, beautiful woman who looked like she had been cut out of a swimwear magazine stood beside him. They were holding hands. Nearby, two children were playing by the promenade wall.

'Uh, hi.'

'Come and meet Isabella.'

There was nothing in the world Grace wanted less right now, except perhaps for a tractor and muck spreader to come driving past and shower her with cow dung. Even then, it was a close thing.

'Oh, sure,' she called, wishing with all her being for a sudden invisible wall to appear in the middle of the road and make their meeting an impossibility.

Isabella was so beautiful she could have stopped traffic. The closer Grace got to the woman who had claimed the vacant heart she had left behind, the more beautiful she became. By the time Grace stood on the promenade before them, Daniel beaming as though introducing his current to his ex was the most normal thing in the world, and Isabella grinning a Vogue smile that made Grace feel she had been shot down and shot down hard, Grace felt like she had morphed into Rumplestiltskin over the course of a few steps.

'It's lovely to meet you,' she said, wondering whether *I'll cut out your heart and lock it in a tower* might not be a more appropriate opening salvo.

'This is Grace Clelland,' Daniel said, indicating her with a flourish just in case Isabella was unsure to whom he might be referring. 'A friend from school.'

'It's nice to meet you too,' Isabella said. 'Daniel has mentioned you before.'

Grace's ears burned. She wondered just what Daniel

might have said. Surely not that he was her first.

'All good, I hope?' Grace said, giving Isabella the chance to reply with, 'No, he told me you dumped him to go off to university, leaving him brokenhearted with a ring in his hand. Are you satisfied with yourself?'

When all Isabella said was, 'Yes, of course,' it was something of an anticlimax.

'I'm just visiting for the summer,' Grace said, as Isabella continued to watch her. She tried to get a glimpse of the woman's hand, to see if she was wearing the ring Daniel had long ago offered to her, but it was clasped too tightly in Daniel's for her to get a decent look.

'Visiting family?'

'Friends. My family moved away a long time ago.'

'So Daniel said.'

Did he now? 'I'm working in the Blue Sands Café,' Grace said, wondering as she said it why Isabella's eyes compelled her to lay her soul bare. Perhaps that was why Daniel liked her? 'I needed a break from city life. It was starting to get me down.'

Isabella was still watching her. 'Is that right?'

'I had some problems at work, trouble with a boyfriend, a couple of other setbacks….' Grace clamped her mouth closed before she started to tell Isabella about the in-growing toenail she'd had cut out last year.

'Well, you'll find peace here in Blue Sands for sure,' Isabella said, sounding like a lifelong local. 'It's a lovely, relaxing place. If you need a shoulder, or just someone to talk to, come and find me in the Low Anchor. We'll share a bottle and a chitchat.'

'Ah, sure. Sounds nice. Um, anyway, I'd better get back. I just popped out for a minute.'

Grace managed to draw her eyes away from Isabella to look at Daniel, standing beside her. He was grinning and nodding as though delighted his ex and his current were set to be such great friends.

'Lovely to see you again,' Daniel said. 'It's nice to have you back around. A familiar face and everything. So many leave and don't come back.'

Grace wanted to be sick. She was just about to make her escape when one of the kids wandered over, did a quick spin of Daniel's right leg and then looked up at Grace, a frown on her little face.

'Who's this old lady?' the little girl said, eyes wide with innocence.

Isabella gave a laugh that could have come from a songbird. Daniel patted the girl on the head. 'Less of the old, Angelica. This is Grace Clelland.'

'This was Grace Clelland,' Grace said clumsily as she backed into the street. 'Now it's just a woman late for work.'

The horn of the bus made her do a weird sideways spider-jump, arms lifted at right angles to her sides. The bus that had braked sharply less than an arm's length away gave a hiss of hydraulics. The driver's window slid down and an irate face leaned out.

'Watch where you're bloody walking, won't you?'

Grace could only mumble an apology. The driver shut the window and the bus pulled off, rumbling along the promenade road. Daniel and the kids laughed, and Isabella put a hand over her mouth as though to catch a secret.

'I'd better get back,' Grace mumbled around a mouthful of utter humiliation, then turned and scurried off before anything could happen to ruin her life further. From behind her she heard Angelica asking her mother an innocent question: 'Does she know she just stepped on some dog mess?' but Grace was out of earshot before she could catch the answer.

18

COMPANION

SHE KNEW HER FIGURE WASN'T PARTICULARLY impressive, but all the spinning classes had been good for something. The swimsuit was a size small, but it wasn't restrictively tight, and she'd checked that she didn't bulge in any embarrassing places. She'd never be a model like Isabella, but she could go for a swim without feeling like a whale.

With the sun going down, the water was losing what heat it had collected during the day. Grace winced as she waded deeper and the little waves sloshed up her body. Then when one larger swell rose right up to her shoulders, she gave up trying to ease herself into the water and just kicked off, ducking down, letting the sea engulf her.

She came up a few feet away, kicking hard, moving out through the gentle water. Once the initial cold shock had gone and her body had adjusted to the temperature, it felt magic. With the sun low in the sky and the few early season tourists gone home, she was free from any disapproval, and let herself relax as she swam out, feeling her muscles stretch and contract as they pushed and pulled her through the gentle swell.

After ten minutes or so she paused, treading water. She was a fair way out now, with deep water below her. Lit by the evening sun, the Mourning Lady was off to the north, Sharker's Rock still some way out further to the south. The beach looked miles away, even if in reality she was probably only two minutes' swim from having sand under her feet, but in water too calm for surfers and too cold for other evening swimmers, she felt utterly alone, and for once, at peace.

Along the top of the promenade, the lights of the pubs had come on. During August the tourists would spill out of the doors onto the promenade, laughing and drinking, but June and most of July still belonged to the few locals who came down in the evening for a quiet drink. Through the lit windows of the Low Anchor she could see a couple sitting at a window table, a woman who could have been Isabella leaning over them, taking a food order.

She was happy for Daniel, really. She would be happier still if Isabella was more of a troll, perhaps missing an eye or with a scar or something. Short, dumpy, a limp. But really, she was happy for him. She had left; he had moved on. It was the way things were, the way things should be. In some ways, despite her problems, it had been a mistake to come back. You could never truly relive the past; there were too many variables, and if the past you were attempting to replicate had been idyllic, you were doomed to failure from the outset. All you could do was attempt to make a new future, one that took the best aspects of the past and added new elements to the mix.

She swam a little further out, almost as far as she dared, until she started to feel the rise of the bigger Atlantic swells no longer deflected by the Blue Point headland. The thrill of swimming into deep water gave her a rush of excitement, but she lingered only a couple of minutes before starting the swim back into the bay, aware that the ocean was not a beast to be tested. As a teenager, she had seen too many helicopters, too many lifeboats sent to pick up tourists who'd been fooled by the water's glassy surface into going out too far.

Soon she began to feel the occasional brush of sand beneath her feet, so she slowed herself and started to tread water again. The year's longest day had passed just a week before, and even now at nearly ten o'clock the beach was still illuminated in a calm orange glow. Clouds had come in along the horizon to hide the sun as it set, but it still felt like a spotlight was falling over the cove. Grace kicked, moving around in a gentle circle, taking in the cliffs rising around her, marveling at how small she felt, and how little it bothered her.

She was about to turn back to the beach when something bobbed out of the water nearby.

At first she thought it was some kind of ball, perhaps having floated out from the beach. Then it moved, big eyes blinked, and the grey seal dropped out of sight.

Grace smiled. She spun around, looking for it. It reappeared a few metres away, in the direction of the Mourning Lady. Grace called out to it, but the seal made no reaction. It watched her for a few moments, then dropped back into the water.

For several minutes she trod water while the seal appeared and disappeared around her, perhaps playing, perhaps wondering what on earth she was doing out in the sea so late. Finally, with the cold starting to creep, Grace swam into the shore and climbed out, brushing drops of salt water off her body. The sun had set now, and a gradual darkness was falling over the sea. A little way offshore, she caught sight of the seal again. She wondered momentarily if it might do something fantastical, like lift a flipper and wave—she considered saying so to Joan anyway, just for a laugh—but it just watched her for a short while, then, perhaps understanding that its brief playmate had given up and gone in, it dropped into the water and was gone.

Grace walked up to the foreshore where she had left her towel, now only a shadow in the falling darkness. Beyond the promenade, the sound of music drifted out across the beach, and bodies moved inside the windows of the Low Anchor.

Grey seals weren't uncommon visitors to Blue Sands. Sometimes in the winter they would drag themselves up onto the beach. It had been some years since Grace had last swum with one, though. She remembered it clearly. It had been the summer she had met Daniel.

'Are you going to bring me good luck again this time?' she whispered, as she sat on a rock and wiped herself dry. Even as she said it, though, she wondered whether meeting Daniel had been good luck or not. After all, things hadn't turned out quite the way she had hoped.

From up on the promenade, she heard the sound of laughter. A group of young locals had brought their drinks out from the pub and were sitting on the wall above the beach. With a smile Grace wrapped her towel around her shoulders and headed up the gravel access track, wondering if there was anyone she knew.

19

OLD FRIENDS

'WHAT'S YOUR ANGLE?' MRS. OLDFIELD SAID, PATTING Daisy as the huge Golden Retriever slumped over her legs like a giant blonde blanket.

'My angle?'

'You've got to have an angle, otherwise your design won't stand out,' Mrs. Oldfield said.

'Can't you just make something artistic, like you did for Jason?'

'Look, there's a big difference between art and design, not that those fools who run the school boards would know. Art is expression, a projection of self. Design is representation, suggestion.'

'Oh.'

'In other words, advertising. You design something that you want people to take note of, so that they'll remember you or buy your products. At least that's what the online course said, and I signed up for that because of their silly dog logo. So, what's it to be? What's your angle?'

Grace gave a little shake of her head. 'Uh, dolphins?'

'You want the café's logo to have a dolphin on it? Since when have dolphins ever been seen off Blue Sands Cove?'

'I imagine if you went out far enough—'

'Far enough that you'd no longer be able to see the café. Too far. What else?'

'Crabs….'

'Dear, you're advertising a café, not a clinic.'

'I saw a grey seal the other night. It was watching me from the water. What about that?'

Mrs. Oldfield didn't look convinced, but she shrugged anyway. 'Better, but I'm not sure. I'll draft you some designs so you can take a look.'

'That would be great.'

It was Grace's day off, so after thanking Mrs. Oldfield for her help, she left the tidy house on the corner of Upper Blue Sands' little housing estate, and walked down to the small high street for some retail therapy. With the exception of one small supermarket, there wasn't a lot on offer in the way of essentials, so she bought herself a couple of gossip magazines, a block of fudge and a coffee, and sat on a bench in the little village green to eat them. Not far up the street, the tiny primary school she had once attended was just finishing for the day. She watched parents gather by the gates to collect their children, who bounced around with the excitement of those knowing the school holidays were a few short days away.

The collection took less time than Grace's nostalgia-tinted memory remembered, the number of local kids barely a fraction of what there had been twenty years ago. She had noticed too how barely half of the houses on the estate looked lived in, the majority now given over to holiday homes. It had been heading that way back when she had lived here, but now the wealth gap between the cities and the country was taking over. The likes of Hedges and Daniel with their successful local business were becoming fewer and fewer. She was the norm: the locals leaving the village in order to find their fortune. Most, however, stayed gone. It was unusual to come back.

A young mother was steering two children towards the swings in the village green's centre. As she passed Grace, her eyes widened, and she made a fish-like gesture with her mouth, as though too surprised even to utter words.

'Grace?' she said at last. 'Grace Clelland? No. It isn't you. It surely isn't. I mean, I saw you sitting here, and I thought, no it's not her. But it is, isn't it? It really is you. Isn't it?'

Grace smiled. Becky Rendle. Unkindly known behind her back as Motormouth. The awkward, garrulous girl who had always been the class monitor or prefect or librarian, or just about any duty that was going, and had always had an awful lot to say about it. The first to raise her hand in class, to last to leave when the bell rang. Irritatingly studious and attentive, she wasn't a girl who had ever been bullied because no one could be bothered to pick apart her complex personality. She had been everyone's and no one's friend at the same time, a pervasive, overbearing presence.

'Becky Rendle?' she said, before remembering Joan's revelation. 'Wow, it's lovely to see you.'

Becky puffed out her chest with pride. 'It's Becky Hedge now. I'm surprised you haven't heard. We had quite the celebrity wedding.'

Grace couldn't for the life of her imagine why, but perhaps Hedges had used some of his lottery money to hire acrobats or even a magician. While her personality appeared intact, Becky had blossomed, the braces gone to reveal pearl-white teeth, her skin so flawless it could have been put through an Instagram filter, makeup done so expertly Grace wondered if Hedges had provided a budget for exactly that. Certainly, whatever fairy dust Blue Sands had to blow about, a fair bit of it had billowed Becky Hedge (nee-Rendle)'s way.

'Uh … congratulations.'

Becky patted her stomach. 'And we're trying for one more.'

Too much information. Grace just smiled. 'That's fantastic. Hedges must be quite the—'

'Stallion.' Becky let out a long breath as she smiled. 'Oh yeah. It's like the more successful his business becomes, the more of a demon he is in bed. Like the two are connected.'

I'll request Joan cancel the pasty order. 'I'm pleased for you,' Grace said. 'And Hedges. I mean, Steve.'

Becky lifted her fingers and pushed her eyelids apart. 'Can you see the bags under my eyes? I'm getting hardly any sleep.'

Please stop. 'It must be a nightmare.'

Becky chuckled. 'Yes, and no.'

'So, what are your children's names?' Grace blurted, almost jumping up off the bench in an attempt to change the subject.

'Riva and Dearin,' Becky said, giving a general nod in the direction of the children and little indication as to which was which. Grace remembered both Hedges and Becky had been regularly seen lugging doorstop-sized fantasy novels around. 'They're boisterous, just like their father.'

'Are you living here in the village?' Grace asked.

'Yes, just up the street there. Number 19. We've renamed it Red Rock Lodge.'

Suitably awkward yet somehow reflective of their combined personalities, their conversation made Grace reluctantly envious. The former Number 19 was on an outer corner of the estate, with a windswept view of farmland and rolling hills, a third floor and the biggest garden on the estate, one which encompassed the entire neighbouring plot. With Suncrust Pasties, Hedges was clearly doing very well indeed.

'That's a lovely house,' Grace said, with real sincerity. 'Are you planning to paint it red?'

'Ha, the council said no.'

Small mercies. 'That's a shame.'

'We're thinking to have a stone wall built outside, though. Maybe we'll paint that.'

'I, ah, look forward to seeing it.'

'Are you staying down here long? You should come over for dinner one time.'

'Only if pasties are off the menu.'

'Ha, they're not allowed in the house. Steve gets his fill for lunch, but I don't like all the butter.'

Grace couldn't help but grin. Becky had been known at school for her butter sandwiches, cut as thick as cheese. Many had said they were the cause of the pimples that had often blighted her. Now, though, her skin was flawless fashion-magazine perfection. Cutting butter out of her diet had clearly done her some good.

'I'd love to come round,' she said. 'I'm here for the summer. I'm helping Joan out in the café.'

Becky's smile dropped. 'Poor Joan. Such a terrible thing. I've helped her out a couple of times myself, but Steve likes me working behind the scenes, doing the accounts. I hope she's handling it all right.'

'She's making the best of it.'

'She always was that type. Better her than me. I would have fallen apart, even with Steve's powerful arms to hold me.'

Grace wondered how she could refer to Steve in such a way without a hint of irony, sarcasm, or even jest. She considered asking Becky how much Steve could press, but was too scared of the answer.

'Right, I'd better go chase those two terrors down,' Becky said, glancing over at the swings, where one of the children had managed to scale the frame and was now hanging off the top bar. 'Lovely to see you, Grace. I do hope we meet again soon. Nothing like bumping into an old friend.'

As she hurried off, Grace felt a warming sensation spread through her, the way it did with the first bite into the crisp crust of a freshly baked pasty. Becky was right. And despite the underlying melancholy she still felt like the cold bottom layer of a pond, she was slowly beginning to warm up to this place and its eccentricities. Everything had changed, yet at the same time, nothing had.

Stuffing another piece of delicious local fudge into her mouth, she stood up and headed for the road.

20

TRAINING

THE SUN WAS JUST TOUCHING THE HORIZON AS GRACE wheeled Joan across the road and up a little concrete ramp onto the promenade.

'Do you want to go onto the beach?'

Joan shook her head. 'No, here's fine. We have a good view and it's warmer up here.'

Grace activated Joan's wheel lock and then sat down on the edge of the promenade wall. She unwrapped a bag of fish'n'chips and handed it to Joan, then took another for herself out of the bag. Joan lifted a chip to her mouth, but Grace shook her head.

'Wait a minute,' she said. 'We need to have a toast.'

'What for?'

Grace pulled a box of wine out of the bag and set it on the wall. She unwrapped a pack of paper cups, took two and filled them with wine.

'What's this?'

'Pinot Noir. It's good.'

'I meant this cup,' Joan said, lifting it up and turning it around to reveal a logo. A swirling line wrote The Blue

Sands Café, while above it was a grey circle with eyes and whiskers. 'Why's it got a picture of an old man on it?'

'It's not an old man. It's a seal.'

'It looks like an old man.'

'Well, it's getting dark. If you see it in the light you'll be able to tell it's a seal.'

Joan frowned. 'Where did it come from?'

'I got it made for the café. It's your new logo. I was talking to some people about how we needed a proper identity if we were going to increase business. We can put it on mugs and t-shirts, maybe even over the door—'

Joan shook her head. 'Ah ha, no chance. At best we'll look like a wildlife sanctuary, at worst like a nursing home.'

'But I thought—'

'Nope. Not happening. I appreciate the effort, I really do, but please tell me you haven't gone and ordered anything with this printed on them.'

Grace gave a forlorn shake of the head. 'No. Only these cups. They're a prototype model. I wanted to surprise you.'

'Well, you did.'

'So you don't like it then?'

'I'm afraid not.'

Grace fell silent. While she would admit that in the gloom the logo did appear a little more like a black blob than she would have liked, in the sunshine she had thought it okay. But if Joan didn't like it, Mrs. Oldfield would surely be happy to tweak it.

Joan patted her on the arm. 'I appreciate the effort,' she said again. 'Thanks for trying. Mum's got her mind made up, though.' Joan popped a chip into her mouth. 'Quick, these are getting cold. What were we going to toast?'

'Tomorrow is the first day of the school holidays,'

Grace said. 'We should see a wave of tourists like never before.'

Joan lifted her cup. 'Not if we're wearing t-shirts with this logo on them, we won't. Cheers.'

Grace had forgotten just how much she liked the mornings in Blue Sands. Up around seven as dawn was breaking on a clear, cloudless day with a tickly breeze in the air, it was still too early for most except a few dog walkers and delivery vans. Grace, wearing jogging gear, did a couple of laps of the foreshore, the soft sand building up a gradual power in her legs that road running couldn't do. Then, so exhausted she wasn't sure she could have ridden on the flat, she took the bike from where she had left it against the hedge at the bottom of Melrose Hill, climbed on and made a sudden surge for the start of the slope.

As expected, she barely made it to the first corner before her strength gave out, but it was better than nothing. If she was going to win the Melrose Hill Bicycle Race, she needed to be in better shape than ever.

Instead of giving up or heading back down for another try, she climbed off the bike and pushed it up the rest of the hill until it flattened out half a mile up. Grace propped her bike against one of the picnic tables in the viewing area and sat down, still breathing hard. She took a bottle of water out of a holder strapped to her waist and downed most of it in a single swallow.

The cove looked immaculate at this time in the morning. The tide was low, the stretch of golden sand out to the waterline glistening in the morning sun. The breeze was typically British, not quite warm enough to be pleasant, but the weather forecast was predicting temperatures touching thirty for the next couple of weeks. It was set to be a glorious beginning to the summer holiday. Grace had already seen a number of camper vans and cars with loaded roof racks heading for the campsites around the village. Many of the campers were yearly regulars, and over the years had become as familiar as old friends, showing up at the beginning of August then hanging around for the rest of the month before sadly departing shortly before the school holidays ended. Teenage holiday romances had abounded, in retrospect the heartbreak over the last few days of August worth the joy of the preceding weeks. Joan in particular had regularly fallen head over heels with some lad or other from the campsites, only to then break the poor boy's heart when he showed up the following year, hoping to rekindle their summer love.

'What goes on in 2008 stays in 2008,' a sage fifteen-year-old Joan had once told Grace while sitting in the shadow of the promenade with a bottle of White Lightning open beside her. '2009 is a new hunting season.'

Grace was still sitting on the bench, fondly reminiscing when a familiar figure cycled into view. Jason, his face soaked with sweat, pedaled the last couple of metres then collapsed sideways onto the grass.

'Are you all right?' she said, as he groaned like a dying man, before disentangling himself from the bike and rolling over. He stared at her for long seconds, his chest heaving. Then, composing himself, he wheezed, 'Nine minutes fourteen seconds. Best yet.'

Outwardly Grace tried to look impressed as she nodded, but inwardly she was pleased. It took the average person around eight minutes just to walk Melrose Hill, so Jason was still some way off the record. He was, however, a lot closer than she was.

When he had recovered enough to stand, he got to his

feet and sat down at the adjacent picnic table. With a grin, he nodded at Grace's bike.

'I see we're in competition.'

'Two minutes, fifty-nine seconds,' she said.

'For real?'

Grace shook her head. 'No. I had to push. But I'll be there. You'll be watching the soles of my shoes on race day.'

'A challenge, is it? I love a challenge.'

Suddenly remembering Jason's request at their last meeting, Grace forced a loud belch. Jason just watched her with amused interest.

'You should get some Gaviscon for that,' he said. 'Sounds like you have a bit of acid reflux.'

'Um, thanks.' She stood up. 'Listen, I—'

'You don't have a quick minute?' he asked, suddenly jumping up.

This was going to get awkward. 'Oh, is that the time?' Grace said, glancing down at her watchless wrist. 'I have to hurry.'

'Wait, I just wanted to ask—'

'Sorry, no time. Joan's a slave master, and I have to um, floss before I go. I haven't brushed my teeth for days!'

'I know a good dentist if you need one. You remember Eddie Byrne from school—'

'I'm good!'

Grace grabbed her bike and pulled it up, jumping on in the same movement. She was pedaling for the top of Melrose Hill before Jason could say another word.

The hill dropped sharply, and in moments Grace knew she was going too fast. The pink BMX's gears were in decent order, but the brakes less so. Grace pulled on the rear brake and felt the wire give under the pressure. With a sudden burst of acceleration, she plummeted down Melrose Hill like an out of control rollercoaster car.

Trying not to panic, she gently worked the front brake, but felt it slipping as it tried to grip the wheel. It was slowing her just enough to make the turn around the Singing Rock, but she would need the long promenade to slow her. And if something was coming the other way—

The protruding field entrance came up quicker than she could have believed. She hacked sideways, narrowly avoiding plowing into the gate, using her feet to try to slow her down. She came around the corner, thankful that there was little traffic this early in the morning, and even fewer people. The road was clear, the road was clear, the road was clear—

The woman appeared out of nowhere, jogging quickly into the incline of Melrose Hill, hair tied back under a baseball cap, tight lycra revealing an impressive figure. She looked up for one second, squealed with horror and dived into the hedge. Grace, fearing a collision, tried to swerve out into the middle of the road. The bike was going too fast. It jerked, throwing her forward into the hedge.

She might have gone right through to the field on the other side if a hawthorn bush hadn't decided to enmesh her. Grace tried to struggle free, but everywhere was pain. Behind her, someone was asking if she was all right, and all she could do was groan because speaking caused a thick, thorny branch to scrape at her stomach.

'Hang on, I'll go and get some clippers,' came Jason's voice. She heard the other, asking again if she was okay. It took her a second to place it, but when she did, she wanted to close her eyes with embarrassment and wish the bike had thrown her all the way over the hedge, into the field beyond, or even better, into an entirely different reality.

'Are you okay up there?' Isabella said again.

21

SURPRISES

'Mum's got another bottle of Dettol up at the house,' Joan said. 'Let me know if you think you'll need it.'

'I feel like a pin cushion.'

'You look like one. What on earth were you thinking? You grew up here too. That hill is lethal. Jason said you did a total dive-bomb.'

'I lost the rear brake and the front was a bit spongy.'

'Come on, Grace, spill. That's a load of rubbish.'

Grace sighed. 'It's actually true, but I was trying to get away from Jason. I went too hard down off the top.'

'Why don't you just tell him you're not interested? Although I'm not sure why you wouldn't be. He's kind of cute in a certain friend's-little-brother kind of way. And it's not like you're beating them off, is it?'

'Thanks. He's just not my type.'

'Well, wait until he asks, and then tell him.'

'I suck at putdowns.'

Joan rolled her eyes. 'At least you get the chance.'

'I'm sorry.'

Joan patted her arm, careful to avoid a couple of

vicious scratches. 'It's okay. Just relax, Grace. Stop worrying so much.'

'I'll try.'

Joan chuckled. 'I can't believe you nearly wiped out Isabella. Daniel came in earlier to tell me to let you know she's fine, just a little shaken. He took her to the doctor for the scratch on her arm, just to make sure there was no infection.'

Grace rolled her eyes. 'Seriously? And people complain about the NHS being abused. I've seen cat scratches worse than that. And it's only because she was fussing over me that she got it. If she'd just waited for Jason, nothing would have happened.'

'I think several people need to calm down,' Joan said. 'But yeah, slight overreaction. He treats her like a princess.'

'Well, she does look like one.'

'You're starting to turn green.'

'That's not jealousy. That's the poison from all those thorns. You know, the hundred or so that got me that I didn't burden the local GP with.'

'You'll know better next time. Listen, I have to get back to the café. Are you going to be all right? Take the day off. Mum's off today, but that's okay, we've got a part-timer coming in for training.'

Grace reached out for Joan's hand. 'Sorry, Joan. I'm being kind of useless at the moment. I'll make it up to you, I promise.'

'I'm happy enough with you just being here,' Joan said. 'It's been a magical summer already, and it's just getting started. Are you going to be fit for the barbeque this weekend?'

'I'll do my best.'

Joan headed back to the café, leaving Grace to mope around the chalet feeling sorry for herself. The scratches that seemed to have covered every square inch of her body were pulling her skin tight, making it sore. For a while she just sat around, reading or staring out of the window, but after a while the boredom began to set in. She remembered the mantra they had used as kids, that seawater could fix anything.

She decided to go for a swim.

She wasn't in the mood for being seen, however, so she climbed up the cliff path to the south, wincing with each step. Instead of heading out to Sharker's Rock, she took a fork leading further south, over the top of the headland and down into the neighbouring valley. Here, a grey sand, mostly shingle beach was accessible only via a steep path, meaning it was usually deserted. Grace climbed down, feeling more peaceful with each step as the curving crescent of deserted beach came up to meet her.

The sea was a calm lake. A couple of seabirds bobbed just offshore, before taking suddenly to flight, engaging in a brief squawking argument and then flapping off towards the headland. Far out to sea, a fishing boat moved imperceptibly slowly across the horizon.

Grace stripped down to her swimsuit and walked to the water's edge. As always, it was crisply freezing at first, but once her body had become accustomed to it, the water's caress made her feel better. She swam out a little way until she could no longer feel the rocks under her feet, treading water as the hawthorn scratches loosened.

Peace. Solitude. Silence.

She breathed in the sea air, wishing she could stay like this forever. She did a gentle circle, taking in the headlands, looking past Sharker's Rock to the Mourning Lady just visible across the bay beyond. Out along the horizon, the fishing boat barely seemed to have moved.

'Nearly there!'

Grace turned at the sound of the distant voice. Two small figures were descending the cliff path. They were moving quickly, the woman in front of the man, both laughing gaily as they went, their voices a soft, loving lilt even if most of their words were inaudible.

They were both naked.

Grace stared. Her eyes weren't sharp enough to recognise them yet, but from the way certain parts ... jiggled ... she could tell they were ... older.

Panicking as they reached the bottom of the path and began to step across the stones towards the narrow stretch of grey sand, Grace looked around, but she was totally exposed. There were no nearby rocky outcrops she could hide behind, and the sea was flat calm. All they would have to do was look up and—

'Grace! Is that you? What are you doing down here? We didn't know you were a convert to this kind of thing.'

With a heavy heart, Grace now recognised them. Belinda and Ron. Joan's parents. She considered taking a deep breath and seeing how far down she could swim before releasing it again.

She was far enough offshore that certain parts remained out of focus if she didn't concentrate too hard, but they were making no attempt to hide anything. She now remembered old pub rumours that this was a nudist beach, although she'd never seen any proof, nor heard of any. It was another one of those things you laughed about over a few pints on a Saturday night.

Now the proof was hanging freely in front of her. Joan's mum lifted a hand to wave, making other parts shake. 'Grace? Are you all right out there? If you've gone a bit deep, Ron can swim out and help you. He might look like a hippo but he can swim like a fish.'

'I'm fine,' Grace called, wondering whether she could swim as far as the fishing boat still sitting on the horizon. Or failing that, the southern tip of Ireland. 'I just got a few scratches from a little accident this morning, and I didn't want people to see.'

'Oh, Joan told us about your accident. When will you learn, eh? You always were a bit impulsive. Well, you enjoy your swim. We're going to have a little run about and then I'll get the sandwiches from the car. You will join us for lunch, won't you?'

'Sure,' Grace called, hope drifting away like the wispy cirrus clouds.

~

'I apologise for them,' Joan said.

'Pass me the wine. If I drink enough perhaps I'll recover my sight.'

Joan couldn't help but grin. 'I would have mentioned it if I'd thought there was a risk of you going over to Penworth Bay. But you know, why would you swim there when you could swim at Blue Sands?'

'Because I look like the guy out of Hellraiser!'

'Ah, you're overreacting. You can barely see anything.'

'That's because I was in the sea for so long my skin dissolved.'

Joan could barely keep the grin off her face. 'Mum said you had a lovely lunch. Did they wear clothes?'

'T-shirts. Because they said they were worried about burning.' Grace rolled her eyes. 'I wanted to burn. I prayed for fire. Once, your dad got up to adjust his towel.' She squeezed her eyes shut and winced at the memory. 'I wasn't expecting it.'

'She makes a good sandwich, though, doesn't she?'

'It's not funny.'

'Was it sausage?'

'Shut up. Ham and cheese.'

'Oh. Could have been worse. I so wish I could have seen your face.'

'I was trying to tear it off. In particular my eyes. Is that a regular thing?'

'They got into it last year. Mum's gone all new-age since the menopause. Decided she wanted to reignite their marriage, and Dad's up for anything. And with their planned move, they've been getting down there pretty regularly.'

'In many ways it's a good thing they saw me. It maybe encouraged them to be more … restrained.'

Joan grimaced. 'Yeah, that's a theatre show I wouldn't want to see.' She twisted round in the chair. 'Come on. Let's get some meat on this fire.'

'Is that meant to be another joke?'

The barbeque was crackling away in the chalet's little garden. Grace, glass of wine in hand, went back inside and retrieved a wrapped package from the sideboard near the sofa. She carried it back outside and handed it to Joan.

'Here. This is Mrs. Oldfield's second effort.'

Joan sighed as she took it. 'Graceful, I really appreciate this, but—'

'Just open it and have a look.'

With another sigh, Joan did so. She held up a tea towel with the café's name on it and a series of ripples above and below it.

'What's this? Corrugated iron? We're not a shed company.'

'It's supposed to be the sea. Don't you like it?'

Joan grimaced. 'I just don't see how this is going to help us.'

'When people see the logo they'll think of the sea. It'll make them want to visit Blue Sands and sit outside your café all summer long.'

'It's more likely to make them think of the café at B&Q with all the screaming kids eating sloppy ice-cream while their dads shop for chainsaws.'

'Do B&Qs have cafés?'

Joan shrugged. 'I have no idea.'

'So you don't like it then? I can try another idea—'

Joan put up a hand. 'There's something else I need to tell you.'

'What?'

'Sophie from the Gourmet Garden must have got wind somehow that Mum was thinking to sell up. She put in an offer. It's way over what Mum planned to ask, enough that she can afford the little café over in Plymouth that she had her eye on. You know, her pet project while Dad works. That's probably why Mum and Dad were mucking about butt naked over at Penworth Bay. She's planning to accept.'

'She can't.'

'Why not?'

'She can't let Sophie have a monopoly on the cafés. She'll just change the name to something generic like Gourmet Garden Two and sell the same generic food she sells now.'

'Have you eaten at the Gourmet Garden? It's anything but generic. At least, not according to the menu. Lime-infused lobsters, and all that.'

'I'm refusing to out of loyalty to you and your mum.'

'That's nice, but before you knock it, you probably

should.' Joan smirked. 'Perhaps you could invite Jason out on a date there.'

'Shut up.'

'Go on, I dare you.'

'Seriously?'

Joan had a mischievous gleam in her eyes. 'Okay, here's a challenge. You ask Jason out on a date, and then take him to the Gourmet Garden's late-night gourmet-whatever that Sophie does. Then come back and tell me that the food sucks, and that we have no chance of stopping her from achieving her world domination.'

'Are you sure?'

'And in return, I'll talk to Mum about your t-shirts, and see if I can get her to hold off on any decision until at least the end of summer.'

Grace was definitely drunk, because even though she was sure in the morning she would regret it, right now it seemed like a really good idea.

'Deal,' she said, holding out a hand.

22

DATING

It was a beautiful sunny day outside, but inside the Blue Sands café, thunderclouds were brewing.

'It's your lunch break, Graceful,' Joan said. 'Go and do what needs to be done.'

Grace, standing by the sandals and hats rack with the intention of burying herself in a fit of tidying for the next couple of hours, glanced back and scowled.

'I'm not hungry.'

'Yes, you are. I let you off yesterday, but you have no excuse today.'

Belinda was adjusting t-shirts on a rack in the corner. 'What needs to be done?'

'Grace has a massive crush on Jason.'

'I do not.'

'Yes, you do.' Joan glared at Grace.

'Oh, how lovely,' Joan's mum said. 'Such a nice boy. Every time I see him, I want to pat him on the head.'

Grace scowled as Joan laughed into her hand and then nodded at the door.

When Grace walked into J's Surf Shack, Jason, wearing a Quicksilver vest, was lifting a heavy longboard up onto a rack, giving her a full view of his muscular torso. All angles and slabs of meat, he looked like he had just broken out of a stone egg. If she found him attractive it would certainly solve a few things, but no matter how hard she tried, she couldn't shake the Jason-from-school image which invaded her thoughts every time she looked at him. He might be buffed like a marble statue, but he was still the diminutive book nerd with the nervous tick who had taken her library card once or twice every couple of months.

'Hey,' she said, swallowing down her pride.

Jason looked around, giving her a nod without any kind of self-consciousness about the amount of male flesh on display. 'Grace. How are you doing?'

'Fine,' she croaked.

Jason turned back to the board and with a grunt managed to hook it back into the rack, the muscles on his shoulders and back rippling with the effort.

'Take a look around,' he said, the awkwardness of the other day seemingly vanished. Perhaps he had gone off her? 'Or is there anything specific that you're after?'

Grace took a step forward. 'Ah….' *Do it for the café.* 'Um … I wondered….' *Don't be scared, you muppet!* 'I wanted to check out Sophie's Gourmet Garden, you know, to take a look at the café's competition. But I didn't want to go alone. So, I wondered if … you'd like to go with me.'

There. The words were out. They felt like traitors laughing and dancing on her tongue. Grace stared at Jason, waiting for his reaction, hoping she didn't appear constipated or in any other kind of pain.

Jason frowned for a moment, then shrugged. 'Sure,' he

said, just as a bell tinkled over the door. 'Hang, on, let me just serve this chap.' He looked past her shoulder. 'Hey, guy. Anything in particular that you're after?'

'My wax.'

Grace turned at the sound of the low, powerful voice as Jason walked past her to the counter. The man standing there wore a Burton hoodie, the hood up, the strings pulled tight. Large sunglasses covered his eyes, and he wore a light wind-cheater balaclava which covered his mouth and nose. Grace stared, unable to move. She felt like she was looking at a movie star, or even a ghost.

Jason reached under the counter and took out a package wrapped in brown paper. The stranger put a twenty-pound note on the table and slid it across.

'Keep the change,' he said, in that same low voice, before swiping the package off the counter and putting it into his pocket. In a moment he was gone, pushing out through the doors.

Grace stared at Jason, who shrugged.

'Was that … him?'

'Billy, yeah. He comes in from time to time. Always dressed like that. Orders his wax from the USA, reckons it's better. Could just get it off Amazon I suppose, but I think he likes to support local businesses.'

The rumble of a starting engine came from outside. Grace ran to the window in time to see a transit van pulling away from the curb.

Grace looked back at Jason. Something hung in the air between them which was slowly dissipating. An air of cool, of mystery. Grace's fingers were tingling, as though she'd been close to an electrical charge.

'The Masked Surfer.'

She realised she was staring at Jason, who just gave an

awkward shrug. 'I suppose that's what some people call him. A bit cheesy, if you ask me.'

'And you have no idea who he is?'

'Nope. If he wants to wear that getup, that's all good by me. A bit weird, I reckon, but that's his deal, isn't it?'

Grace was still staring at the door. 'Who could he be?'

Jason laughed. 'I reckon he's some old greengrocer called Alf who doesn't want people to know his identity because he reads loads of spy magazines in his spare time and thinks it's funny to get people going.'

'You read too many books.'

Jason shrugged again. 'Yeah. Used to, yeah.'

She turned to look at him. He had a strange look on his face, like a dog that had lost its master and was looking for some kind of instruction. Grace had completely forgotten the thread of their previous conversation until Jason said, 'So, um, this dinner date? Ah, what time?'

Joan was sitting in her chair on the promenade, a pint of beer on the stone wall in front of her. 'Is that what you're wearing? Seriously?'

Grace shrugged. The hoodie was a little oversized, and the brand wouldn't impress anyone outside of TK Maxx or the job centre queue, but it was comfortable.

'I'm trying not to make a good impression.'

Joan rolled her eyes. 'You didn't brush your hair.'

'Or my teeth.'

'Grace!'

'What?'

Joan handed her a pack of Wrigley's. 'At least chew one of these. I'll take them off your wages.'

'Do you have garlic flavour?'

'Don't be so reluctant. You might like him.'

'If you had a little brother, it would be like dating him. He's shorter than me for a start—much shorter—and he used to work in the school library. He used to have bucked teeth.'

'Yeah, and now he's completely ripped, a gun surfer, and has teeth so straight he could star in a Colgate advert.'

'He's still Jason from the library.'

'Stop being so shallow and give him a chance.' Joan grinned. 'And remember our deal. If you survive the first date, I'll talk to Mum.'

Grace frowned. 'Am I really being shallow?'

'Just a little. You show up lamenting your pathetic love life, pining over your lost love who's now got a perfect family, and then you act like a dick when I kindly try to set you up with a friend.'

Joan had a grin on her face. Grace rolled her eyes. 'All right, I'll try.'

Jason was waiting on the promenade across the street from the Gourmet Garden. He looked a little awkward as he stepped forward to meet Grace, on Joan's insistence now wearing a tasteful summer frock which exposed her legs below the knees. Jason was wearing an O'Neill t-shirt which still had the creases from being recently taken out of a packet, and a pair of jeans with brand-designed ripped knees.

'You, ah, look nice,' he said, making Grace cower inside. She had promised Joan, but nothing felt natural about this at all.

'Thanks. So do you. Shall we go over?'

'Um, sure. Did you book?'

Grace frowned. 'Do we have to book?'

'I don't know.'

They headed across the road. The Gourmet Garden looked like a regular café and shop on the ground floor, complete with postcard racks, ice-cream counter, and chalkboard drinks menu, but the second floor had an extended veranda, its wall lit up with tastefully arranged fairy lights. From above them came the sound of gentle conversation and laughter.

'You got a table?' Jason said to the young lady standing behind the shop counter. 'Um, for, ah, two?'

The girl picked up a clipboard, ran a finger down a list, then turned and called to someone out of sight through a staff entrance behind the counter. An affirmative cry came back, then the girl turned and nodded.

'Follow me,' she said.

She led them up the stairs and indicated a table by the wall at the top. Three other better tables were empty, but theirs was uncomfortably close to the stairs, and the light glaring out.

'Can't we sit over there?' Grace asked.

'I'm sorry, we have a booking from nine,' the girl said.

'But it's only seven-thirty. We'll be done by then.'

Glancing at Jason, he looked more hopeful than crestfallen, as Grace had expected. The waitress, however, shook her head. 'Gourmet Garden has a one night, one booking policy,' she said. 'In future, it would be best to make a reservation.'

'No sittings then, like at school,' Jason quipped as they sat down, giving Grace an uncomfortable reminder of their school days, of the way Jason had seemed to dribble when he laughed.

The waitress handed them the menus, pointed out a couple of specials, and left.

'Are we going Dutch?' Jason asked. 'I mean, I'm happy for you to be all feminist and take the bill, but I thought I'd ask.'

Grace forced a smile. At least it would be easy to refuse a second date. 'Dutch is fine,' she said. 'I'll have a sautéed cod in light batter with primrose oil pan fried potatoes.'

'Nineteen quid for fish'n'chips? How much is Joanie paying you? Talking of Joanie—'

'Welcome....'

They both looked up at the woman standing over them who had appeared out of the lights glaring up the stairs like a witch out of a puff of smoke. Grace gulped. It had been some years since she had seen Sophie Baker up close, but the woman whom her mother had once referred to with distaste as 'the local siren, leading husbands astray,' had lost little of her once infamous sultriness. Jason, adding more ammunition to the one-date cutoff, stared at her like a puppy at its mother.

Sophie's hair was like a glossy black curtain, her half-lidded eyes ringed by anemone-like eyelashes which seemed to waver in the breeze like the tentacles of some poisonous creature calling men to their doom, while her full—probably Botoxed—lips parted in the smallest of smiles.

'Is this your first visit to the Gourmet Garden?'

'Yes,' Jason squeaked, his voice suddenly unbroken, reverting him to a thirteen-year-old on the cusp of puberty.

Grace just smiled, wishing Sophie would cast her spell and leave them alone.

'Today's special is the locally raised ground pork shoulder patty served with a freshly baked bread roll and fresh garden salad.'

'I'll have that,' Jason squeaked.

Grace channeled Joan's defiance as she met Sophie's predatory gaze. 'And I'll have the fish'n'chips.'

Sophie's eyes narrowed. 'You mean the sautéed cod in a light batter?' she said with a hint of menace.

'Yes, that.'

'Drinks?'

'Two pints?' Jason suggested, glancing at Grace, who quickly nodded.

'We serve only Californian wine,' Sophie said. She leaned down, revealing cleavage which had definitely been enhanced, and flicked over a page of the menu to reveal a wine list.

'Twenty-eight quid for house red?'

'The house is a 2014 vintage,' Sophie said, sounding mildly hostile.

'We'll have a glass of that and a mineral water,' Jason said.

'Very well. Please be patient. Everything is cooked to order.' Sophie scooped the menus up with a hand manicured with crimson nails so long she likely used them for scraping the souls from the hearts of sailors. As she departed, Jason leaned across. 'Eight quid for a glass of wine. Can you believe it? You bang the mineral water and I'll top you up,' he said. 'I've got a flask in my pocket.'

'A flask? What's in it?'

Jason grinned. 'Malibu. Isn't that what girls drink?'

For the first time, the tension broke, and Grace found herself laughing. 'They do now,' she said. 'What about you?'

'I've got another flask in my other pocket. Rum and coke.'

'I feel like I'm at a beach party.'

Jason grinned. 'Well, we are, more or less. Listen, since you're here, I really wanted to ask you—'

'Entrees,' came a voice beside them, as the waitress appeared at the top of the stairs.

'We didn't order any—' Grace began, but the waitress shook her head.

'Entrees come with every meal.'

'What is it?' Jason asked.

'Pan-fried, freshly gathered whelks in a garlic butter sauce,' the girl said, putting down a plate between them. 'Enjoy your meal.'

She was gone before either could protest. Both Jason and Grace stared at the plate.

'Water snails,' Jason said. 'So fresh I can see one still twitching.'

Something nudged Grace's leg. She was about to pull away when she felt the cold touch of metal. She reached down and took the flask Jason was passing to her out of view of the waitress lingering at the top of the stairs.

'On the count of three,' he said. 'One, two … three.'

Both lifted their flasks and drank. Grace winced at the sweetness of the Malibu, but as a little buzz began to kick in, she started to feel better.

'Right,' Jason said. 'Rock, scissors, paper for who goes first.'

'You are joking?'

Jason smiled. 'Nope. If we're being forced to pay for these, we've got to eat them.'

The Malibu was giving Grace a little confidence. She spied a small whelk by the side which she would force down if she had to, but there was no way she could possibly lose. Beginner's luck.

'Rock, scissors, paper!' she said, holding out her hand as Jason did the same. Grace frowned. 'What the hell is that?'

Jason, holding out his hand in a C-shape, shrugged.

'Tiger's claw. Beats everything. But you can only use it once. Eat up. And I get to pick. You can eat the massive one in the middle.'

'Not fair!'

'You agreed.'

'Not to be cheated, I didn't.'

'Go on. Loads of people eat them.'

Grace stared at the whelk. It was curved like a snail, and had the appearance of a snail. The garlic butter was just decoration. She glanced at Jason, who was watching her with expectation. Perhaps if she just tried to swallow it in one go—

She grabbed a fork and speared it before she could chicken out. Then, with one swift motion, she stuffed it into her mouth.

It was like eating a hard lump of garlic-flavoured rubber. She got two chews in, then an image of a snail popped into her mind, and she was done. She retched, jerking forward, the half-chewed whelk flying across the table towards Jason's lap.

Like a seasoned cricket pro he was on his feet in a moment, batting the thing away with the palm of his hand, sending it sailing high over the veranda to land in the street below. He sat back down, looked at her, and grimaced.

'I think I might have got it into the river. You know, set it free and all that.'

Grace could only laugh. She was still laughing when Sophie reappeared, announced the formal names of their food, and then put a hamburger in a bun in front of Jason and a plate of fish'n'chips in front of Grace.

As Sophie retreated down the stairs, Grace popped a chip into her mouth, then said, a little too loudly to Jason, who was still staring wide-eyed, 'Stop staring at her tits.'

Jason grinned. 'I can't help it,' he said. 'They fill the entire night sky.'

They decided to pass on dessert, instead heading over to the beach. The tide was low, the sea a distant rumble. With no breeze, the air was warmer than usual for late July. They found a sheltered spot on the sand below the promenade, just out of the glare of a street light.

Grace was feeling a little tipsy, having polished off Jason's flask of Malibu. Having grown to like him over the course of the evening, she found herself up for anything. She'd never actually done it on the beach, and had only ever heard bad things from people who had—that it was never like the movies, there were always stones, and the sand got everywhere—but now that she was in the position where it might happen, she found herself not against it. Jason was nice enough, if a bit short, and it would certainly make a change from the unwanted celibacy her life had assumed.

Jason produced two cans of beer from somewhere, holding one out to Grace. 'Cheers for a fun night,' he said, popping his can and holding it up. 'I can't believe we got charged nine quid for those whelks.'

Grace laughed. 'We didn't even order them. I now know why I've never eaten there before. I don't think I could afford it more than once a year.'

'I had a good time, though,' Jason said, leaning a little closer. 'I was a bit nervous at the start, but you know, it was fun.'

'Yeah.'

Grace realised she was leaning closer too. It would only take one swift movement by either of them to close the deal, and then the night could take over. Jason was frowning, though.

'Listen, I know this might be weird, but I've been looking for a chance to bring it up.'

'Bring up what?'

Jason gave an easy smile, re-establishing the moment Grace had thought was about to pass. 'It's just, I wasn't sure how to ask.'

It'll be fun, Grace thought. *I'm a little drunk, but it'll be fun. I might regret it in the morning, but probably not that much. Why not? Better to regret what you do than what you don't. Isn't that right?*

'It's Joan,' Jason said. 'I wanted to ask you about Joan.' He smiled again, his face cracking, and suddenly tears were streaming down his face. 'I'm goddamn obsessed with her. I just don't know what to say.'

Grace felt like she was in the middle of a bubble that had just been popped, and now she was freefalling to earth with no way of stopping.

'Huh? Joan?'

'When you asked me out for dinner, I figured it was a good chance to ask you about it. I've been trying, but I'm just scared, and I guess I needed a little sauce to get the words out. She's just so cool, and whenever I talk to her I feel really relaxed, but you know, she's in that thing, and I don't want her to think I like her out of sympathy—'

'The wheelchair. She's in a wheelchair.'

'Yeah, that. I don't want her to think that I'm just being some kind of Mother Theresa or UNICEF or whatever—'

Grace could only smile as the absurdity of the situation made itself clear. She had been moments away from getting down to it on a cold beach with Jason from the school library. She felt every drop of the Malibu as she started to laugh.

'You know you just talked yourself out of a shag?'

Jason looked horrified. 'No offense, but you're like … Grace from school.'

'What's that supposed to mean?'

Jason grimaced. 'You're nice and all that, but I'm not into sporty girls. And you were like the sportiest.'

'Isn't that a bit odd coming from you?'

Jason shrugged. 'Just trying to keep myself in shape. Not getting any younger, am I? Joan won't be interested much longer. You reckon I have a chance?'

Grace laughed. 'You won't know until you ask her, will you? Tell you what. I'll give you to next weekend, and if you haven't done it, I'll do it for you.'

Jason was practically bouncing up and down. 'Really? Man, you're so cool, Grace. I wish I was as cool as you.'

Grace could only smile. As she watched the pure delight on Jason's face, she wondered what kind of whelk life was likely to throw her next.

23

THE LIBRARY

Joan's happiness left Grace feeling bittersweet. On the one hand, Grace was delighted because Jason and Joan made such a great couple, but on the other she was disappointed because they were rarely apart, and in many ways she felt like she had lost her best friend. Jason would show up at the café in time for Joan's lunch break, then take her wheeling off along the promenade for a picnic on the beach, or fish'n'chips out of one of the takeaways farther along the strip. Grace would stay behind with Belinda to deal with the lunchtime rush, feeling both happy for her best friend but frustrated at the same time.

'It'll be your turn soon,' Joan's mum would say, patting her on the arm, although Grace felt further away from any kind of life-defining relationship than ever.

August ticked around, the local campsites filling up and leaving Grace exhausted after long afternoons of scooping ice-creams and carrying cream teas to the tables outside the café. By the time she got back to her chalet at night, she was often too exhausted to even think about going back out to the beach or to the pub. Many nights she would just take a cup of tea out to the little table on her back patio and sit thinking about the day, listening to the occasional cry of a gull and the distant rumble of the beach.

At least now she felt at peace. The constant battery of emotions which had engulfed her in Bristol on a day-to-day basis had abated here by the seaside. Mornings were the best, when she got up early, took a walk along the beach and then made her obligatory attempt to cycle up Melrose Hill. She was still no closer to her goal, but seeing the shadows shorten over the beach as the sun rose, it was heavenly. There was no place on earth she would rather be.

'How about we increase the size of the ice-creams?' she said to Joan, as they waited for the first customers, one morning on the second week of August. 'Give them a cheeky extra half-scoop. Word will soon get around.'

'We'll make no money.'

'But you'll get them in the door, and then they'll buy other stuff.'

'I'll ask Mum about it, but I can't see her going for it. She'll want to make as much money as possible before she sells up.'

Outside, the Suncrust Pasty van pulled up. A couple of minutes later Steve Hedge pushed through the door, dragging a trolley of pasty boxes behind him.

'How are you both this fine morning?' he asked, a larger-than-usual grin on his face.

Joan smiled, and Grace just shrugged. 'What's up with you?' Joan asked.

Hedges set down the trolley and picked up a cardboard sign that had been lying on top of the boxes. 'Any chance you could put this up in your window somewhere?' he asked, still grinning.

Grace took the sign and turned it over.

We serve Suncrust Pasties
WINNER – *Cornwall's Choice* Awards

'Congratulations,' Joan said. 'When was this?'

'Last weekend,' Hedges said, clapping his hands together. 'First prize in the foodstuffs category. Apparently it wasn't even close.'

'What's Cornwall's Choice?' Grace asked. 'Is that some kind of magazine?'

Hedges shrugged. 'Dunno. An online blog or something. Doesn't really matter. First prize is first prize.'

After bringing in another load of pasties, Hedges bade them goodbye and went off to continue his deliveries. Grace waved the signboard at Joan.

'That's it,' she said. 'We need to win an award.'

'For what?'

'Best café.'

'And how do we do that?'

Grace clicked her fingers. 'Leave it with me.'

She needed to get online, something she had been staunchly against during her weeks back in Blue Sands. It wasn't hard to avoid it; there was no cell phone reception in the cove apart from a couple of shaky Wi-Fi signals, so if she wanted to use her phone she had to walk up Melrose Hill to the village. However, staring at a phone screen for long periods had never been Grace's favourite way to spend her time, and she didn't want to ask Joan if she could borrow her laptop. The only option she had left was to use the public computers in the small Upper Blue Sands combined library and museum.

Set among trees on an outcrop of land at the top of the cove's valley, the library had the best view of the cove below that wasn't in some rich non-local's garden. The ground floor was set into the hill, but from the rooftop terrace you could just make out the orange line of the beach at low tide. A young man in spectacles looked up as she entered through a glass sliding door.

'Is it okay if I use the computers?' Grace asked as the man adjusted his spectacles and gave her a welcoming smile.

'Sure,' he said. 'Although you're supposed to make an ID card.'

'Okay, right.'

He handed her a sheet of paper and a pen. Grace filled in her details, then passed the sheet back across the counter. The man looked at it, his eyes widening.

'Grace Clelland?' he said, looking up. 'I thought it was you.'

The museum-library had always been run by the Davis family when she was a kid. She remembered Paul Davis from school, but the spectacles aside, there was nothing familiar about him. She guessed it could be him, but the shy, quiet kid with the bland face that no one ever really noticed had grown into a mature, intelligent man.

'Do we know each other?' she asked, just in case she was wrong.

He smiled. 'Paul Davis. We were in the same class at

school? We sat next to each other in Mrs. Minke's biology class in the fourth year. Don't you remember?'

Grace gave a slow nod. Mrs. Minke had been a school terror. You had to sit in alphabetical order, and speaking between pupils unless given specific instruction to do so was forbidden. You had to pronounce her name with a long I sound to make it into "Meenke" or risk drawing her terrifying wrath. Occasionally a new kid would pronounce it with a hard I. They never did it twice.

In Mrs. Minke's class you were expected to sit straight and face the front. Even turning towards other kids could have been seen as a sign of delinquency, so it wasn't a surprise Grace had rarely spoken to Paul, even across an entire school year. Talking had been strictly prohibited.

'I do remember you, but not very well, I'm afraid. How are you doing?'

Paul shrugged. 'Good. I work here full time, but it's the only place in Blue Sands which doesn't get crowded with visitors, so it's quiet.' He handed a card across the table. 'Here you are. Use your I.D. number to log in, and the password is Blue123.'

'Thanks.'

The computers were a lot older than Grace had hoped, and she grabbed a couple of magazines to flick through while waiting for screens to load. As soon as she could, however, she began searching for bloggers and local websites, emailing all of them with her request.

It was a simple one: to visit the Blue Sands Café for themselves, and then (hopefully) write something nice about it.

She was still hard at work when Paul came over. 'Excuse me, Grace?'

'Yeah?'

'It's ten past six. I need to close up.'

Grace nearly jumped out of her seat. She had been emailing bloggers for the last four hours, and still had a couple of dozen on the list she had compiled.

'I'm sorry, I lost track of time.'

'It's fine.'

She gathered her notes and quickly logged off. Paul apologised for seemingly pushing her out, but Grace felt a pang of guilt about keeping him so late. Apart from one old lady who had come in a couple of hours before and requested a book on pruning fruit trees, she had been the only customer all afternoon.

On the way home, she stopped in to see Mrs. Oldfield. The old art teacher gave her a speculative eyebrow as she handed across the latest logo design, one of the mourning lady printed beneath the café's name.

'What do you think?' Mrs. Oldfield said, as Grace held the t-shirt up in front of her.

'It's … nice.'

'What does it make you think of?'

The idea had felt like a good one, but as Grace stared at it, she knew what Joan would say. Resisting the urge to put on Joan's voice, she said, 'It makes us either look like a rock climbers' club or a support circle.'

Mrs. Oldfield gave a curt nod. 'I didn't want to say it, but you've stolen those words right out of my mouth. What would you like to try next?'

24

ACTS OF HOSTILITY

'IT'S UNFAIR, IS WHAT IT IS,' JASON SAID, AS JOAN PATTED him on the arm. Nearby, the barbeque was cracking quietly, three burgers nicely browning.

'It happens,' Joan said. 'Big fish, small pond and all that.'

'It should be for locals only,' Jason grumbled, shaking his head. 'What's he coming down here for?'

Grace listened with a mixture of emotions. Jason's point of view was fair, but on the other hand, the Melrose Hill Bicycle Race was a public race and, since it was being televised, it was only right that it be open to anyone who wanted to enter. Who could tell a former pop-star they couldn't join if they wanted to? After all, it was great publicity and would bring loads of extra tourists to the area for the weekend of the beach gala.

And that it just happened to be Mike Anderson, he of the buns and the Adonis of Grace's spinning class, on the comeback trail after his injury … wasn't that perhaps a sign of fate?

'He's got a solo album coming out,' Jason moaned.

'Some radio friendly rubbish, and he figured he'd promote it by entering a bunch of local races around Devon and Cornwall, with copies given as raffle prizes. I have enough beer mats already. I don't need any more.'

'Weren't you into Westlife?' Joan said. 'I seem to remember kids taking the Mickey out of you at school.'

Jason pouted. 'It was Backstreet Boys,' he said. 'And that was school. This is now.'

Grace flipped the burgers as Joan consoled Jason. 'Food's ready,' she said, wishing her cheerfulness didn't seem too genuine. Part of her was really looking forward to seeing Mike. They'd never really spoken at her spinning class, but she'd caught his eye a couple of times. Perhaps there was something there….

'Excuse me?'

Grace looked around as the back door to the next chalet along opened and an elderly woman stepped outside. She leaned on the door frame and reached across the partition fence to tap on Grace's patio door window with her walking stick.

'My Gerald is trying to get some sleep. Do you mind keeping the noise down? This is the third time this week and I really don't want to have to call the council.'

'I'm sorry,' Grace said, trying not to look at the face Joan was making out of the old woman's line of view.

'And the smell of that silly fire, it's making our whole chalet stink,' the woman continued. 'Don't you know about the carcinogens in fire? A microwave is much safer. You really should show more consideration for the people around you.'

'Again, I'm sorry,' Grace said. 'We'll finish it off quickly.'

'Do you want me to get you a bucket of water?' the

woman asked, then turned and shuffled back inside without giving Grace time to answer.

'Made a new friend there,' Joan said, as the old woman's door closed. 'Happy summer.'

'She arrived two days ago,' Grace said. 'She's already told me off for playing the TV too loud, even though the chalet doesn't have one. I think she's hearing voices.'

'Could be a ghost,' Jason said. 'You know, some of the houses back here are supposed to be haunted. There was an old prospective mining tunnel back in the hill there, which apparently collapsed around the turn of the eighteenth century. I know a song about it—'

'No!'

Jason clapped his hands together, stuck one foot out and leaned back on the heel. 'There was a merry old man from Trevose, Trevose, who had a spot on the end of his nose—'

Joan lifted a hand to silence Jason as the neighbouring chalet's back door opened again and the woman reappeared. This time she was holding a mixing bowl filled with water. She carried it up to the little fence separating the two narrow back gardens, and held the bowl out to Grace.

'Take this quickly, dear. My strength isn't what it used to be.'

Grace had just removed the burgers, and caught in the respect-thrall of an older person, she took the bowl without question.

'Hold it low to the coals, dear, then pour it gently. That should reduce the amount of guff you get billowing up into the air.'

Grace was aware of Joan and Jason sniggering behind her. Feeling like she ought to protest but held in a strange tractor beam of control, she did as commanded, dousing the flames with the water, then stepping back to avoid getting a faceful of charcoal steam.

'That's better, dear,' the old woman said. 'Let me have the bowl back, if you would. And do you have a fifty pence?'

As Grace handed over the bowl, she said, 'Fifty pence? What for?'

'The water, of course. The bills are astronomical down in this part of the world. I don't know how the council lets the water board get away with it.'

Joan and Jason couldn't stop laughing as they sat together on the promenade wall. As Grace sipped at the pint Jason had carried over from the pub, Joan shook her head.

'Oh, that was hilarious. She made you pay for the water.'

'I only had forty pence in change. I told her I'd drop another ten over in the morning. Thanks again for the pint, Jason.'

'No worries. Do you need me to spot you that coin?'

Grace shook her head. 'No, I'm pretty sure I've got one hiding in a glove box in the car or something. Otherwise I can, you know, just go to the bank.'

'If I find tomorrow night's till off by ten pence I'll be docking your wages,' Joan said, smiling. 'I guess that means our weekly barbeques are finished.'

Grace gave a defiant shake of her head. 'No chance. We'll just carry the stuff over to the beach. There's no law against it. And you know what? I'm going to make them bigger and better. Open to everyone. Let's make this a summer to remember.'

'Sounds good. Oh, looks like it's going to rain. Anyone

up for another pint indoors? Come on, Graceful, are you ready to break down the final frontier?'

Grace looked across the street at the steps leading up to the Low Anchor's entrance around the back. From open windows on the second floor came the sound of music and laughter.

She had run into a lot of familiar friends and retread a lot of old ground during her weeks back in Blue Sands, but she had never managed to bring herself to step inside the pub. Once it had been her favourite place in the village, particularly in the summer when the tourists were about and it was buzzing with energy. Now, though, it was run by her ex-boyfriend and his perfect wife, and the thought of it made her feel uncomfortable in a way nothing else did.

'I think I'll get an early night,' she said.

As the rain became heavier, they finished their drinks and headed back across the road. At the foot of the steps, Joan said, 'Are you sure?'

Grace nodded. 'I can't face it ... not right now.'

'It's all good. Jason and me will be in there until last orders if you change your mind.'

'Thanks.'

She watched them heading off, laughing and joking with each other as Jason pushed Joan's chair around to the disabled-access entrance at the rear. Part of her was insanely jealous of their happiness, but that was becoming an increasingly lesser part as the days passed. Mostly she just felt happy for them, and it gave her more reason than ever to somehow save the café. It was Joan's legacy; without it nothing would be the same.

By the time she got back to her chalet, it was pouring with rain. She fumbled in her pockets for her key, but it was proving elusive. Just as her fingers crossed over it, the door to the adjacent flat opened and a rectangle of light appeared. Grace, huddled beneath the narrow overhang of her doorway, stood in silence as the elderly lady who had shut down their barbeque party appeared, huddled under an umbrella.

'Come on, Gerald,' she said. 'Let's have you out of there. Can't have you going to sleep with a full bowel, can we? You'll be passing wind all night.'

A little tipsy, Grace had to slap a hand over her mouth. She stared in forced silence as, grunting, a little pug jumped down from the doorstep, wandered over to the chalet's narrow patch of grass, and spread his legs apart while the women held the umbrella over him.

'That's it, get it all out. You know I can't stand that cabbage smell, especially now I have to keep the windows shut. Good boy, Gerald. Now make sure you wipe your feet on the way in.'

With another grunt, the little pug wandered back inside. The elderly woman leaned over the lump of brown on the grass. Then with a sigh and a shake of the head, she reached down with a trowel held in her free hand and scooped it up. She glanced at it a moment longer, then flicked it over the fence into Grace's front garden.

Still without having noticed Grace standing barely an arm's length away, huddled in her dark doorway, the old woman turned and shuffled back inside, shutting the door behind her.

Grace stared in disbelief at the dark shadow of the pug's dump on her little patch of grass.

It felt like a declaration of war.

25

RESEARCH

As Grace fell off her bike and collapsed onto the grassy verge in a state of near-exhaustion, she glanced at her watch. When her eyesight stopped wavering she felt a momentary rush of excitement: it was her best time yet.

She climbed up onto the nearest picnic table and sat gasping for air as her racing heart began to slow. Eight minutes and fifty-five seconds. It was an honourable attempt, but nowhere near enough. Jason reckoned he'd broken eight-thirty ('although I was guessing from the clock because I forgot to start the timer'), but she had looked at Mike Anderson's Instagram in the library yesterday, and he was boasting that he expected to break seven minutes. His thighs had never felt more powerful, he said, his butt like a piston engine ready to propel him to race and then chart success.

Grace found she was going off him.

From the picnic area, Blue Sands Cove looked beautiful today. A perfect blue sky, not a cloud to be seen, the sea like a pristine sheet of blue glass. It made all her problems easy to forget.

Her watch beeped. Eight thirty. She climbed back onto the bike, heading back down into the valley, taking it easier this time after nearly hitting Isabella a few days before. As she descended past a couple of dog walkers, she gave Mrs. Oldfield and Daisy a smile, then her neighbour—whose name she had learned was Ethel Dottington—a curter smile as Gerald the pug nosed in the grass verge before cocking his leg over a patch of thistles.

She started work at nine o'clock. Showered and changed, as she reached the front doors at a minute to nine, she glanced over at the beach.

A thick white cloud hung low over the horizon.

Sea mist.

'You see it?' Joan said, wheeling out through the doorway to meet her. 'Better pick something good off the rack to read. Looks like it could be in all morning.'

The unpredictable sea mist, which could roll in any time and completely blanket the coast in a cloud of cold, wet moisture, meant the beach would be deserted most of the day. The mobile families with cars would all head inland to the shops or the theme parks, while those stuck on the campsites would forgo ice-creams and sandwiches for an afternoon playing UNO or drinking in the pub. During high season, while it meant a day of low takings, it often provided a nice breather from endless streams of customers and aching forearms from scooping hard ice-cream for hours on end.

Belinda had taken the day off, but the handful of hikers and dog walkers who stopped for a coffee was barely enough to keep one person busy.

'Here she comes,' Joan said, nodding through the window at the old woman making her way slowly along the promenade. 'That's her, right?'

'Public fun spoiler number one,' Grace said.

Ethel came tottering across the road, Gerald waddling behind her. She tied the dog up outside then entered, glancing at Joan and Grace behind the counter without so much as a nod in greeting. Then, after a quick glance at the postcards, she made her way to the newspaper rack.

'She was in here yesterday too,' Joan said. 'She went through every one, then wandered out again without buying a thing.'

'Not like she needs one to wrap up her dog mess, is it?' Grace whispered back.

They watched Ethel nose through the papers for a while, before a group of hikers came in for a breakfast order. A few minutes later, after the group was seated and plates of egg and bacon had been delivered, they went back into the shop to find Ethel had gone.

'Look,' Joan said, wheeling around to the newspaper rack and pulling a badly folded paper out of the rack and rearranging it. 'She doesn't even put them back properly. Mum doesn't care because we barely make anything off newspapers, but I think it's taking the Michael, quite frankly.'

'Perhaps we should dump a bucket of food waste onto her back lawn,' Grace suggested.

'Don't tempt me.'

With the sea mist staying in past lunchtime, meaning the beach would likely be empty even if it cleared, Joan decided to have a "wild moment" and close the café for the afternoon. A few minutes later, Jason appeared in a bright red, battered Volkswagen Beetle and whisked Joan away for an afternoon of shopping in Truro. Grace regrettably turned down the offer to "be the pusher so that J can carry the bags", deciding instead to head up to the library and continue her emailing blitz of local news sites and bloggers. With the mist turning to warm, August rain, the library had attracted several elderly locals and a handful of tourists. Grace hid herself away in a corner booth while they bombarded Paul Davis with questions.

About five o'clock, Paul came over to tell her the library was about to close. Outside, the rain had become torrential, leaving the valley a grey watercolour, Blue Sands Point and the cove visible only as indistinct smudges.

'Do you need an umbrella?' Paul asked, as she peered out of the doorway. 'We get dozens of people leaving them behind. I can fish you one out of the back room.' He smiled. 'Do you have any kind of brand preference?'

Grace laughed. 'Do you have a Burberry?'

'Actually, we do. It's got a bent spoke, but otherwise its fine.'

He went behind the counter into an office and reappeared a moment later with a tartan-designed umbrella.

'It has to be worth fifty quid,' he said. 'A tourist left it behind last year. Never came back for it. Funny how umbrellas seem to be the ultimate disposable item. Apparently more than thirty thousand get left on the London Underground each year.'

'I wonder what they do with them all?'

'Give them to the Tate Modern to make sculptures, I imagine. I like to think they distribute them to the homeless, but I expect they're all just sitting in a big room somewhere along with a few boxes of mobile phones.'

Outside, the rain was getting even harder, the wind picking up with it, like a January storm which had lost its way.

'Gotta love August,' Paul said. 'Listen, if you don't

want to brave it, I can drop you home. I usually walk but I drove in today, just in case. You learn to predict the weather after a while.'

Grace shrugged. 'Sure.'

'I just need to check the windows and lock up. Can you give me a couple of minutes? There's a little coffee left in the staff filter if you'd like some.'

'Thanks.'

Paul brought her a cup of coffee from the back room which was just warm enough to be enjoyable. She waited in the lobby while he shut down the museum and library. A few minutes later, he returned, pulling a jacket over his shoulders.

'You're wearing a coat?' she said, smiling.

He shrugged. 'Cornish weather. It could be snowing by midnight. Hang on a minute. I'll bring my car around.'

Grace waited while Paul went out into the rain and hurried around to the car park at the building's rear. A couple of minutes later an old Ford Fiesta pulled up outside.

'My wheels,' he said, after climbing out and returning to the lobby. 'It can get sixty on a decent downhill straight, sixty-five if I really push it.'

'Always best to travel in style,' Grace said.

Paul locked up the library and they got into the car. 'Where are you staying?' he asked.

'Down in the cove, in one of the chalets,' Grace said.

'I know the ones. Down that little narrow street past the chip shop?'

'That's it.'

'Got it. Hang on a minute while we power up.'

He gave the engine a little rev, then pulled away. The rain was so heavy they could barely see through the windscreen.

'It must be a little strange coming back,' Paul said. 'I mean, you could travel half the world but Blue Sands would be just the same. The people a little older, but that's about it.'

Grace smiled. 'It's like seeing an old friend. And it's peaceful. The city was starting to drag me down.' Then, thinking back over her own words, she started to laugh. 'Listen to me. You'd think I was an investment banker or a pop star or something. I was working in a café, just letting the years drift by. It's not like I was changing the world or anything.'

'Changing the world is overrated,' Paul said. 'As long as you're happy in your part of it, that's what matters. Blue Sands is all about the history, the people, the sea. You don't need to complicate things.'

'Do you go down to the cove much? I've never seen you down there.'

Paul shrugged. 'From time to time. I live up in the village, but I go down once in a while.'

They were heading down Melrose Hill now. It felt like they were driving down a waterfall. Paul steered out into the road to give a wide berth to Mrs. Oldfield, who was holding an enormous golfing umbrella over Daisy.

'That poor dog looks soaked.'

'She's always out, rain or shine,' Paul said. 'I'll offer her a lift back up after I've dropped you off. I keep a tarpaulin in the back just in case. That dog is like a giant sponge.'

The promenade was deserted, the rain keeping most people inside. Most of the shops had shut for the day, although there were lights on in the Low Anchor. Grace squinted, trying to spot Daniel through the windows, but the rain was too heavy.

'Here you go,' Paul said, turning down the narrow

street and pulling up outside the chalets. 'Yours is not the one with the pink BMX, I take it?'

Grace winced. 'I'm afraid so. It's a relic from my past. I can't seem to let go.'

'If it still works, why replace it?' Paul said. 'Take care getting up the path. You're liable to wash away. Keep the umbrella.'

'Thanks.'

She climbed out, opening the umbrella as she did so.

'Have a good night. Take care, Grace.'

She gave Paul a wave as he drove off, watching the car's taillights meander away into the rain. A moment later he reached the junction with the main road, paused for a moment, then turned left, in the direction of Melrose Hill.

With the rain pouring around her, Grace stood still for a few seconds, watching the road where the car had gone, a strange feeling coming over her, one she hadn't felt in a long time.

26

HEARTSTRINGS

THE SURF WAS ALWAYS GREAT FOR A COUPLE OF DAYS after a storm had rolled out to sea. After a busy day in the café, it felt wonderful to be paddling out on a board as set after set of clean, glassy waves came rolling in. Proudly wearing her Rented from J's Surf Shack wetsuit, Grace sat out the back with the other local surfers, with the sun hanging low in the sky above them.

The strength was beginning to return to her shoulders and back. Waking up the morning after the first couple of decent surfs, she had felt like a steamroller had rumbled over her during the night, but now the muscle ache was reduced to an almost pleasant feeling, the same way she felt after a good spinning session. The first time, it had taken her twenty minutes to paddle back out after the first wave, but now as she dropped out of a ride and pulled her arms through the water, she glided back out through the incoming set as easily as she had done as a teenager.

The sun was starting to set behind her, the light glittering off the wave crests as their faces became shadows. Most of the surfers had gone in now, but Grace hung around, waiting for one last decent ride. Surfing wasn't quite like riding a bike, because the decade that had passed since her surfing days ended had changed her balance, slowed her movements. They were coming back, but she still needed to practice if she had any chance to avoid embarrassment in the surfing competition. Just one more wave—

'Hey.'

She had been sitting facing out to sea, so the voice caught her by surprise. She turned, her heart racing, to see Daniel pulling through the water behind her. He came to within a couple of metres, then sat up on his board.

'I thought I saw you out here. That's a great wetsuit, by the way.'

Grace just shrugged. 'Shouldn't you be working in the pub by now?'

'Isabella's got it, and we have staff on tonight. I couldn't resist the swell.'

'It's good this evening.'

'Yeah. I saw you ride that last wave. Nice turn.'

'Thanks.'

'You've still got it.'

From the way he was looking at her, she briefly misunderstood what he meant. Then he nodded at the board and said, 'You probably need an upgrade. It's a shame about your old board.'

'My dad sold it before they moved. I mean, I said it was okay.'

Daniel looked about to say something else, but a swell was building behind them. 'Here's mine for the evening. Come up to the pub sometime for a chat. We haven't really caught up since you came back.'

'Sure—'

She wasn't sure he heard her before he dropped to his

board and began paddling into the wave. Grace let it pass under her, then briefly saw the back of his head appear as he stood on his board, riding it into the beach. She hoped he might paddle back out, but instead she saw him ride right into the shore before dropping off his board and carrying it out through the shallows. He turned and gave her a brief wave before heading up the beach.

Grace felt a knot building in her stomach as she watched him walking away. So much had been left unsaid, but she remembered he was married now. He had a family.

She had drifted in a little too far. She pulled her board back and ducked just as a wave broke over her. Paddling quickly back out, she sat on her board again in the dusk as the sun dropped below the horizon. A short distance away, a grey head popped out of the water, watching her.

Grace couldn't help but smile. 'Just you and me, now,' she said to the seal.

She caught a couple more waves, then headed back into the beach before it got too dark to see. As she walked up the foreshore to the access ramp, a figure waved at her from the promenade.

'Hey!'

Joan was sitting by the wall, a bag at her feet. Grace walked over and leaned the board against the wall.

'What are you doing out here alone?' Grace said. 'Where's Jason?'

Joan smiled. 'Doing his accounts. He told me you were out there surfing, and I thought it might be nice for us to have a drink together. We've not had much one-on-one time recently since I got together with Jason. I'm sorry, Grace.'

'What for?'

'You're my best friend, and I feel like I've been neglecting you.'

'Nonsense.'

'I saw Daniel out there. Is everything all right?'

Grace started to speak, but suddenly a wave of emotions hit her in a sudden rush. She tried to say it was okay, that everything was fine, but instead she found herself blubbering, shaking her head.

'I don't know what's going on,' she gasped through sobs she thought loud enough to be heard up in the village. 'I thought I was over him, and I think I would have been if he wasn't still here. I can't stand it, Joan. Every time I see him with her or his kids, I feel like that should be me, like I missed out.'

'Grace, it's all right,' Joan said, starting to pull her into a hug, before grimacing at her dripping wetsuit. 'It'll be okay.'

Grace pulled away. 'I'm pathetic, aren't I? I mean, you've had so much to deal with, and I'm making a fuss over this.'

'You have to get him out of your system. Come on, there's only one way to do that. Go and get changed and meet me in the pub in half an hour.'

Grace looked at the bag at Joan's feet. 'Didn't you buy some drinks in?'

Joan smiled. 'Oh, I'll drink these while I'm waiting. Go on, hurry up. There might be half a can of Dutch courage left when you get back.'

By the time Grace got back to the promenade, it was nearly half past ten. Joan, shivering in a jacket now the sun was long set, handed Grace a can of beer and looked her up and down.

'How many times did you change outfits? And you only

needed to wear a hat. No need to brush your hair. We're going to exorcise demons, not pick up.'

Grace felt herself blushing. 'I can't go into a full pub without a bit of makeup.'

'I do.'

'Well, you're in a relationship.'

Joan lifted an eyebrow. 'You think I don't try for my man?'

'I didn't mean—'

Joan laughed. 'Come on, Graceful. Drink up. Let's get inside before my wheels ice up.'

It felt weird to go through the creaking double doors of the Low Anchor for the first time in ten years. Even though Grace was pushing Joan ahead of her like a battering ram, the conspicuousness she felt was almost overwhelming. Through the frosted glass of the inner door she saw groups of people standing around the bar, others sitting at tables, some walking around the pool table or back and forth from the darts board.

'Deep breath, Graceful,' Joan said, then propelled herself forward, pushing the door open with the foot braces on her chair.

A cacophony of sound engulfed them. Grace followed Joan inside, feeling like she was stepping through a time warp. The stools were new, but otherwise the bar looked the same as it always had. The same pictures on the wall of local club teams, the same memorabilia on a shelf above the bar, the same scratched sea buoys hanging from a hook in a corner. And many of the faces were the same too: old Jimmy Trebarwith, a local farmer, sat in the middle of the bar where he always had, his garrulous words as difficult to understand as ever, the Compton couple—Mavis and Don—sat at the far end, drinking the same drinks—a wine spritzer and a Worthington—as they'd always drunk. Crowding around the pool table was the Beattie family, a group of tourists from somewhere up north who came every year, and always wore the same matching t-shirts. Big Lawrence Beattie—the father—had shorter hair than Grace remembered, and Kelly Beattie had filled out a little, her hair showing signs of grey. The three kids were there, too, but the two oldest—a couple of years younger than Grace—were now adults, and the youngest, who had waddled around in the others' wake, now a strutting teenager.

As Joan wheeled herself to the bar, several people turned to greet her. Grace trailed along behind, feeling like a stranger until old Jimmy noticed her and clapped his hands together, expelling a loud guffaw at the same time.

'Well, I never,' he growled. 'Grace Clelland! Is that you, lass?'

'Hey Jimmy,' Grace said, as other faces turned towards her. Within a few minutes she was picking up greetings from old acquaintances, school and family friends. Joan passed her a drink as she fielded questions on her parents' health and what she'd been doing since she went away.

Everything seemed to be going well until she looked up and noticed Daniel behind the bar. He was standing at the end, talking to the Comptons. And beside him stood Isabella, a picture of beauty in a long summer dress, one hand on Daniel's arm as she laughed at something Don Compton had said.

Some things had changed, and suddenly Grace couldn't handle it anymore. She made an excuse to the old school friend she was talking to and hurried out, ostensibly to the toilet, which she bypassed as she ran down the steps and out onto the promenade.

A few people were sitting outside with drinks carried out from the Low Anchor or other pubs further along the strip. Grace wandered along the promenade until she reached the first steps leading onto the beach.

The tide was up now, the storm swell died down, little waves rushing up the sand to lap at the shingle on the foreshore. Grace stood just back from the waterline, letting the chill sea breeze wrap around her.

Far out to sea, the lights of a fishing boat moved across the horizon. Grace watched as it passed behind the outcrop of the Mourning Lady, and briefly made the rock stack visible against the night.

Was this how Lucy Pearce had felt after Peter Trevellian had left for the Napoleonic Wars? Deserted and alone? Heartbroken? Was it worse that her lost love was still alive and well, and as happy as could be with his beautiful wife?

Grace sat down on the sand. She felt utterly miserable, but pathetic at the same time. She was twenty-eight. She should have got over him by now. She needed to stop acting like a scorned teenager, particularly when the whole situation had been her fault in the first place. After a wonderful summer together, she had dumped Daniel. He wasn't ambitious enough for her, and living in Blue Sands for the rest of her life was the worst thing in the world.

As she stared out at the rippling water, she remembered something her old grandmother had once said to her long ago. Her grandmother, God rest her soul, who had spent her youth working overseas as a nanny for diplomats' children in places as exotic as India, New Zealand, Egypt, and the Philippines, had once smiled when an eight-year-old Grace asked her, 'Granny, what's the most beautiful place in the world?'

With a soft chuckle, her grandmother had answered, 'It's right here, at home. But you won't know that for yourself until you've been away and come back again.'

27

RESOLUTIONS

Joan, sitting in her chair with a cup of takeaway coffee balanced on her knees, was clearly tired and hungover, but Jason, in a skin-hugging singlet looked almost homo-erotic as he leaned on his bike. Grace, giving them a wave as she approached, pushing the pink bike in front of her, shook her own drowsiness away.

'Good morning, Graceful,' Joan said, yawning. 'Thanks for calling my parents in the dead of night. Are you really sure this is necessary?'

Grace looked at Jason. 'One of us has to win,' she said. 'We can't let Mike Anderson come swooping in here and win a locals' trophy.. This needs to stay in the village. And if training together is the only way to do it, then so be it.'

Jason grinned, then lifted an arm and flexed his muscles. 'Nothing like a bit of healthy competition.'

'You two are mental.' Joan turned to Grace and cocked a thumb at Jason. 'How'd you know he'd be up for it?'

Grace glanced at Jason and smiled. 'Because he won't want to lose to a woman, will you, Jason?'

'Are you calling me sexist? I'm quite happy for you to win the woman's race.'

'There isn't a woman's race.'

'Well, come second, then.'

Grace looked at Joan. 'See? If he thinks I'm going to beat him, he'll try his butt off. Much as it pains me to admit, I have no chance of winning, but if I can help Jason win, that's all right. But being satisfied with some stumpy little award for being the fastest local isn't good enough. You have to beat the pro to win the tro.'

'The what?'

Grace blushed at the awkwardness of her attempted joke. 'I meant the trophy.'

'Ah, the tro.' Joan looked at Jason. 'Go, um, Jo. To win the tro.'

Laughing, Jason jumped off his bike and ran around behind Joan, leaning her chair back and running a few feet up the hill with her. 'You're Jo,' he said. 'Let's get the tro!'

'Will you two just pack it in?' Grace said. 'I'm trying to be serious here.' She glanced over her shoulder at the Gourmet Kitchen a little way down the street. A teenage boy was outside, sweeping up around the tables on the street level patio, but standing in the doorway, watching him with an almost witchlike intensity, was the black-clad Sophie Baker. One finger rubbed her chin, her talon-like fingernail glinting in the dawn sunlight.

'There's something else I need to tell you,' Grace said, pulling a flyer out of her pocket. It had ripped corners and was torn halfway across. 'I saw this on a lamp post on the way back from the beach last night.'

It was an advert for the Melrose Hill Bicycle Race, the final event of the Bank Holiday Weekend Blue Sands Beach Gala. It had a feature on Mike Anderson, the special guest competitor, and there on the first line was the damning proclamation, *Sponsored by Blue Sands Gourmet Garden Restaurant.*

'She's going to bury us,' Grace said. 'Jason has to win, and he has to win in the café's brand t-shirt.'

'The one with the old man on it?' Jason asked.

'It's a seal. And no, not that one.'

'The crabs one?' Jason sniggered as Joan's fist flicked out to crack him on the arm.

'No, the other one.'

'What other one?'

Grace grimaced. 'The one I'm still working on.'

'We've got like, two weeks?' Joan said. 'Why don't we all just give up and drink away the rest of the summer?'

'Because this is important.'

'To you, yeah.'

Grace looked at Jason. 'And to him. And to Blue Sands. And to you, and the café, and everything.'

'How do you figure that?'

Grace glanced at her watch. 'I'll tell you at work. Come on, let's hurry up because I want to grab a surf after this is done.'

'You're keen, aren't you?'

Grace smiled. 'I'll concede the bike race to Jason, but I'm damned if I'm not winning the surfing competition for myself.'

Jason shrugged. 'I'm one of the judges. I reckon it'll be flat calm anyway.'

They decided to start their practice race from just past the Singing Rock. Jason pushed Joan about halfway up, from where she could see both the starting point and the finish, then walked back down to Grace and climbed onto his bike.

Joan, holding a stopwatch over her head, shouted, 'One, two, three, go!'

Grace went off hard, knowing she had to push Jason if she was going to help him beat Mike Anderson. To her surprise, though, she found herself quickly pulling away as he struggled to keep up. The twice-a-day surfing sessions she had recently been doing had improved her fitness, and she found a burst of adrenaline as she thought about Daniel, wanting to exorcise him from her mind.

Only as they reached the last corner before the top did she start to lose ground. Jason came alongside her just as they crossed the official finish line. Giving each other a high-five, they freewheeled their bikes back down to where Joan was waiting.

'Practically a dead heat,' Jason said confidently as Grace gave him a scowl. 'It could go either way.'

Joan held up the stopwatch. 'It's going one way, Mike Anderson and Sophie Baker's way. You're forty-seconds off Anderson's best.' She pointed down the hill at the Singing Rock. 'One more time.'

Jason went as white as the sea foam. 'Seriously?'

Joan grinned at Grace. 'You drag me out of bed to watch you two sweat your way up a hill and you think I'm letting you off after one little ride? You gave me the stopwatch; that makes me coach. Get back down to that rock *now*.'

'Joan—'

'You will address me as Coach, sir, until I say we're done.'

'But—'

'You'll do it twice more for showing dissent. Move.'

'Yes, Coach. Sir.'

'Yes, Coach, sir.'

As Grace followed Jason downhill, she heard Joan laughing. 'Twice more and you can both have an ice-cream on the house.'

Jason glanced at Grace, then looked back at Joan. 'Jo— uh, Coach … a large?'

'No, a small. You're in training. But if you break eight minutes on the next climb I'll make it a big small.'

Grace was almost too tired to surf, and with only half hour to catch a few waves before starting work, she nearly gave up. However, having seen a couple of decent sets rolling in during her arduous hill training, she ran back to the chalet to get her board, just in case.

To her dismay, by the time she got to the beach, the only waves to be found were out on the reef by Sharker's Rock.

With no time to get out there and back before starting work, she sat down on the foreshore to watch the one surfer who had bothered to go out. As he cut and turned with effortless skill, it didn't take her long to realise she was watching the Masked Surfer, even if his van was nowhere to be seen this morning. With a couple more weeks of practice, she reckoned she'd have the measure of any of the other local surfers, but this guy was on a different level. He would ace the competition without a doubt, but there had been no one on the list whom she didn't recognise either as local or a known talent. Perhaps competitions were below him.

But what about … girlfriends?

She didn't want to act all fan-girl, but as he caught one last wave and then paddled in to the beach, she saw one possible way to help herself get over Daniel Woakes. She waited until the Masked Surfer had almost reached her before standing up and offering a smile of greeting.

'Nice waves,' she said.

He paused, looked about to say something, then just smiled beneath his mask and walked on. Grace felt like he had blown her out. She was still sitting and staring after him, her face smarting with embarrassment, when he turned back.

'I enjoyed the ice-cream the other day. Thanks.'

Then, with a smile, he turned and walked off, leaving Grace staring at his departing back, her mouth agape. As she watched him cross the promenade to a small car park where she saw that his van was parked at the back, she could only give a little shake of her head. Then, feeling like an idiot but unable to control herself, she stood up and shouted, 'What flavour did you have?'

She thought he hadn't heard her. Then, just as he reached his van, he turned back and shouted, 'Honeycomb. My favourite.'

28

ICE-CREAM MYSTERY

Joan gave an exasperated sigh. 'We sell hundreds of ice-creams,' she said. 'We've shifted two tubs of honeycomb in the last week. I mean, how am I supposed to remember everyone I served?'

Grace was adamant. 'It's the key to the mystery. Why don't you have security cameras?'

'We do.' Joan pointed at a little CCTV camera hanging from the ceiling at the far end of the shop.

'It doesn't work. It's not even plugged in.'

'I know that, and you know that, but potential shoplifters don't.'

'It's still not much use, is it?' Grace thumped her hands against her thighs. 'Come on, think. I remember serving two to a kid yesterday. I mean, he could have given it to someone waiting outside.'

'Lawrence Beattie always has honeycomb,' Joan said.

Grace shook his head. 'He's way too tall. And he has a different accent.'

'Maybe he gave it to one of his kids.'

'They're too young.' Grace clicked his fingers together.

'I have an idea. We need to be vigilant, but, you know, it's hard when it's busy.' She leaned down under the counter and searched through a box of odds and ends until she found what she wanted. Holding up a sheet of paper and a pen, she said, 'Every time anyone orders a honeycomb ice-cream, make a note of it on this piece of paper. If it's a local, write their name. If not, try to engage them in conversation, or follow them outside and try to see where they go.'

'So basically stalk them or hit on them?'

'Be subtle.'

Joan sighed. 'I'm not sure what you're trying to achieve with this.'

Grace frowned. 'No, neither am I. But it's important.'

'Why?'

'It just is.'

Outside, the Suncrust Pasties van pulled up, and Steve Hedge climbed out. He went around to the back of the van and unloaded several boxes, which he then wheeled in through the door on a trolley.

'Good morning, ladies,' he said. 'A bit of a scorcher out, today, isn't it? I imagine you'll be busy this afternoon.'

Joan glanced at Grace. Then, with a scheming smile, she looked back at Hedges. 'Thanks, Steve. Do you want an ice-cream for the road? On the house.'

Hedges lifted a bushy eyebrow, then scratched at a sideburn. 'Really? Don't mind if I do.' He set the trolley down and leaned over the ice-cream freezer.

'What flavour would you like?' Joan said.

Hedges frowned for a moment as his eyes flicked over the display of flavours on a sign beside the ice-cream freezer. Then, giving them both a sly grin, said, 'I'm partial to a bit of honeycomb.'

~

'Admit it, Grace, he's the right height.'

Grace, carrying an open box of Mars Bars, retreated towards the café in order to escape the latest round of badgering that had been going on all morning. 'Stop playing around. There's no way it's Hedges. For a start, why would he hire a transit van? He'd just show up in a Suncrust Pasties one.'

'You're looking for holes in the evidence, Graceful. The Masked Surfer is clearly Hedges. You have the hots for Hedges. Just admit it.'

'Just shut up.'

'Excuse me?'

They both looked up to see a plump middle-aged woman leaning over the counter. 'I'm from Sunny Days Out in Cornwall. The blog? I'd like to get a free sandwich lunch set in exchange for a positive review.'

Joan frowned. 'A what?'

'A review.'

'I'm sorry, we don't—'

'Yes, we do!' Grace said, leaning in front of Joan. 'Come through to the café and I'll find you a seat.'

A couple of minutes later, after Grace had sat the woman down at their best corner table near the window and given her a menu, Joan waved her behind the shop counter. 'Grace, what's this about?' she said in a low voice so the woman—currently the only customer in the café— wouldn't hear.

'I'm just trying to get you a little more business,' Grace said.

'Sunny Days Out in Cornwall? Never heard of it.'

'It's a prestigious blog site. They do yearly awards.'

'Is that so?' Joan pulled her phone out of her pocket

and wheeled around the counter. 'I'll be back in a minute. I just need to go up the street and steal a bit of Sophie's Wi-Fi.'

'You know the password?'

'I figured it out. "Number One." Smug old mare.'

'Young lady? I'm ready to order!'

Joan lifted an eyebrow. 'You'd better go and feed our food critic. A quid says she orders the prawn sandwich, since it's the most expensive.'

Joan was glaring at Polly Biggins, the lady from Sunny Days Out in Cornwall, as she stuffed lumps of chocolate cake into her mouth.

'I should take this out of your wages,' she said to Grace. 'She has nine blog followers. Nine!'

'And they might have nine each, and so on....'

'I appreciate the effort, so I'll let you cook me dinner as punishment instead. Oh no, here comes trouble.'

Ethel Dottington, who had been eating a ham sandwich on a corner table with Gerald sitting at her feet, came over to the counter.

'Excuse me, but I heard that lady mention that her cake was included in the lunch set. I'd like to know why I wasn't offered a lunch set when I ordered.'

Joan grimaced. 'Because we only just started doing them.'

'Isn't that against trading standards? Perhaps I should write a letter to the Western Morning News—'

'What cake would you like?' Grace said quickly. 'Chocolate, cheesecake, or caramel shortcake?'

'Cheesecake,' Ethel said.

'The most expensive,' Joan muttered under her breath.

Grace forced a smile. 'Certainly.'

'And I'd like another coffee, since you've been giving that lady free refills.'

'Free refills are only on tea,' Joan said.

'What's the difference? It's all just flavoured water.'

'Free refill coming up!' Grace said.

'I should think so.' Ethel lifted up a dog's bowl. 'And while you're at it, can you fill this with water for my Gerald? Wash your hands first, please. If you get any coffee grains in it I'll never get him to sleep.'

Grace forced another smile. Joan, who had wheeled back out of view of the café counter, was making circular motions with her fingers next to her ears. As Ethel went back to her table, Joan said, 'Mum won't need to sell up come September. At this rate, by then we won't have a business left.'

'Three honeycombs, please.'

'Certainly.'

The grey-haired man stood back as he waited for Joan to serve him. Grace, standing by the café counter, tried to catch Joan's attention, but Joan was pointedly ignoring her. Three days of scribbling down notes and they were no closer to figuring out who the Masked Surfer might be. And Grace's constant pestering for information on whoever even vaguely fitted the description was starting to drive Joan mad.

As the man carried the three ice-creams out of the shop, Grace hurried over to Joan. 'Why were you ignoring me? Who was that?'

Joan laughed. 'Don't worry, that's not him.'

'I know, he was far too old. But he bought three. Who did he give them to?'

'Graceful, you really need to ease up on the panic. That was Frank Davis. Don't you remember him from school? He was the drama teacher.'

'I dropped drama after the second year.'

'Ah, I forgot.'

'Wait a minute. Frank … Davis?'

'Yeah, Paul's dad.'

'Paul….'

'He was in your class at school. He works in the village library owned by his family, remember? It's not going to be him, is it? He probably couldn't lift a surfboard, let alone use one.'

Grace ran around the counter and peered between the racks of buckets and spades out of the window. Frank Davis had carried his ice-creams across to the promenade, where Paul was waiting with an older woman whom Grace guessed had to be his mother.

Grace gave a little shake of her head. There was no way. Paul just didn't have the build for it. But he was about the right height, and some wetsuits were pretty thick.

'It's him,' she said. 'I can't believe it. It's Paul.'

'It's more likely to be me,' Joan said, laughing. 'Come on, Graceful, back to work.'

29

SUSPICIONS

Daisy was taking up the entire sofa as she snored, so Grace was forced to perch on the edge as she showed Mrs. Oldfield the draft of her latest design.

'So, what's this, then, dear?'

'Can't you tell?'

Mrs. Oldfield looked pained. 'Well, no, not really. That's some kind of fish?'

'It's a shark.'

'And it's holding hands with a….' Mrs. Oldfield looked up. 'What is this, exactly?'

'It's the Mourning Lady. The shark is holding hands with the Mourning Lady.'

Mrs. Oldfield fixed her with a firm stare. 'May I ask why?'

'It's a bond. Like a circle.'

'And whatever does this have to do with the Blue Sands Café?'

'It's supposed to represent friendship and connection.'

'But why would a shark be friends with a historical figure that may or may not have even existed? I get what you're trying to express, but, to be frank, you're not doing a very good job of it.'

Grace sighed. 'I'm doing my best.'

Mrs. Oldfield patted her on the arm. 'Stop trying so hard. You're overcomplicating things. Logos and emblems are supposed to be simple.'

'It is simple.'

'You call that simple? No wonder you dropped art at school.'

'I didn't drop art. I just sat at the back.'

Mrs. Oldfield gave a smile that took Grace right back to the classroom. 'Well, somebody has to. We can't all drive on the roads. Someone has to build them.'

'Do you have any ideas?'

Mrs. Oldfield lifted an eyebrow. 'This is your design, so it must be your idea. Think about what you're trying to express. Think about why you came back to Blue Sands, what the café means to you, and what it should mean to others. Then, express that in a simple logo. Bring it back to me and I'll do the rest.'

'We only have two weeks until the gala.'

'Well, you'd best get on your bike and hurry up.'

After her chastening at the hands of Mrs. Oldfield, Grace stopped into a little café for lunch and then headed for the library. She was nervous about bumping into Paul, whom she was now convinced was the Masked Surfer, but at the same time she really wanted to know how her blog search was going, and even though she'd discovered that if she sat outside the pub at night she could get just enough Wi-Fi signal to use her phone. The first time she'd tried it she'd almost bumped into Isabella, who liked to go out for midnight jogs along the promenade after the pub had closed, and always spent some time outside on the patio stretching and warming up.

Paul was sitting behind the desk as she entered. Wearing spectacles, outwardly he looked as far from the Masked Surfer as it was possible for a person to get. As she stared at the curve of his jaw and the width of his shoulders hidden beneath a plain sweater, however, she became more certain than ever. He was Clark Kent, obvious to everyone watching, hiding Superman behind the flimsiest of disguises.

'Hello, Grace,' he said, looking up, and looking a little nervous at the same time. 'How are you doing?'

As he glanced down at his stomach and made a point of adjusting his sweater, she realised she was staring.

'Um, good,' she muttered, wondering why the butterflies in her stomach wouldn't leave her alone. 'I just need to use the net.'

'Sure, go ahead.' He smiled. 'If you can find a free computer.'

With the skies clear and temperatures close to thirty, the library and its connected museum were empty. Grace had seen only Paul's car parked outside, which had made her even more nervous, because it meant he wouldn't be busy. Sooner or later, they would have no choice but to talk.

For now, though, her nerves got the better of her, and she hid herself away in a computer cubicle. To her excitement, Polly Biggins had posted a review of the Blue Sands Café on her blog. Giving both the food and the staff five stars, she had shared it to her Instagram account, where it had picked up three likes, and one comment from someone called Bobsworkaccount: "Sounds nice."

Grace shrugged. Small gains. She checked her email,

and found that a handful of other blogs and online magazines had promised to stop by. Clicking on one to have a look at its details, she stared in astonishment.

South West Secrets, an online magazine with more than ten thousand blog followers, and another twenty thousand on Instagram. A proper big gun in the industry, which offered a yearly summertime dining award. Now that she thought about it, Grace was sure she had seen a notice up in the window of the Gourmet Garden. Clicking through previous winners, she confirmed what she had thought. A Highly Commended, awarded a couple of years ago.

Highly commended. It would be sweet to get one over on Sophie Baker by winning it. Quite how Joan's ham sandwiches could compete, Grace wasn't sure, but on her pseudo date with Jason she had been left unimpressed with the Gourmet Garden's supposed fine cuisine. Perhaps if they added a little more pepper and stuck a sprig of parsley on the corner of the plate?

She pushed back from the computer, mind reeling with ideas, and almost fell off the chair when she found Paul standing nearby. With a pained look on his face, he held up a mug.

'Coffee?' He gave a guilty shrug. 'You're not supposed to drink over here, but, well, no one's around to be offended. As long as you don't spill it on the computer.'

Grace smiled. 'Thanks.'

Paul handed her the cup and started to turn away, pausing at the last moment. 'This is going to sound weird,' he said, 'but I was wondering....' He trailed off. Grace noticed his cheeks redden and a shine of sweat appear on his brow. The confidence she had seen in the Masked Surfer was nowhere apparent, but, she remembered, that was an act. Clark Kent had been a total nerd. The costume was everything.

'What?' she said, as he started to turn away again. She gave him what she hoped was an encouraging smile.

'Ah, I just wondered … if you're not busy sometime this week, do you want to, you know, get some food or something?'

She studied his face for a few seconds, waiting for the butterflies to stop their merry dance in her stomach. What was wrong with her? She tried to picture him spearing through the waves with the wetsuit mask over his face, strong hips and thighs cutting the board back and forth. It was nearly impossible to imagine, but the evidence was there. His height, his shoulders, the set of his jaw; it was him. It had to be.

'Sure,' she said.

30

LOST BOY

'O.M.G. You're going on a date with Paul Davis? You can't seriously think he's the Masked Surfer?' Joan sniggered. 'Where's he taking you? For a picnic on the rocks off Sharker's Point, or out to the back of a whale?'

'Don't take the Mickey.'

'It was a genuine question. I mean, I'd love to have dinner on the back of a whale. Just don't sit over the blowhole.'

'Shut up.'

Joan leaned against the counter. 'Come on, Graceful. No way it's Paul Davis. He's like … a nerd.'

'Jason used to be a nerd,' Grace said, just as the shop's bell went. 'And look at him now. He's buffed as anything.'

'Thanks,' came a voice from behind them. Joan started laughing as Jason, carrying a bag from Haddock Enough Yet?, began to flex his free arm. 'Been working on my tri curls this morning. Can you tell?'

Grace rolled her eyes. 'What do you see in him?'

'I like a man who treats his woman well,' Joan said.

'Chips on the promenade for lunch. How can you beat that?'

'I'll even give your chair a push,' Jason said.

'My knight in lycra armour,' Joan said. 'Look after the shop for me, Graceful. Don't burn it down.'

'Excuse me?' came a voice from the café counter. 'Is this where you order a free reviewer's lunch?'

Joan rolled her eyes. 'Not another one. That's three in the last two days.' She stared at Grace. 'I appreciate your efforts, but can you please stop giving our food away?'

'Excuse me? I'm from South West Secrets.'

'If you want free food, come back half an hour after closing time,' Joan shouted. 'The bins are round the back.'

'Shut up!' Grace hissed. 'That's—'

'The squirrels and hedgehogs usually make a queue, but if you get in there quick you can get first dibs.'

'Joan, no—'

'Well!' came the customer's voice. 'Well I never. In all my time—'

'She's special needs!' Grace shouted. 'Ignore her. Please take a seat and I'll be with you in two minutes.'

She looked back at Joan, who was glaring at her. Jason was sniggering behind his hand.

'Sorry about that,' Grace said.

'I can't believe you pulled the special needs card,' Joan said, narrowing her eyes. 'Only I'm allowed to do that.'

'She has twenty-thousand followers on Instagram!' Grace hissed. 'She's huge.'

'Is that good?' Joan glanced at Jason, who shrugged.

'J's Surf Shack has ninety-four,' he said. 'Was ninety-five last week but my dad decided to go on an internet blackout and closed his account. Twenty grand is pretty good.'

Joan's eyes flared at Grace. 'Well, get in there and serve

her! What are you waiting for? She has twenty-thousand Instagram followers!'

Grace ran back behind the counter, scrambling for her apron. She glanced back at the sound of the door's bell to see Jason wheeling Joan out of the shop.

'Where are you going?'

Joan looked back and grinned. 'I'm going for lunch with my boyfriend. I'm special needs, remember? I can do what I like.'

The damage had been done. The woman from South West Secrets ate her sandwich and cake, then slapped a ten pound note down on the counter and told Grace to keep the change.

'Oh, and as another tip, I'd suggest you train your staff in some manners.'

Grace muttered an apology, her cheeks burning as the woman left. A couple of other customers had overheard, and muttered underhand comments as they got up to leave. Grace leaned over and thumped her forehead on the counter top.

It was futile. Perhaps it was time to give up. Maybe fate had set itself in motion and the café couldn't be saved. Joan was happy now with Jason and was losing interest, and everything Grace had tried had failed. They were losing money, and she was losing her resolve. For the first time in weeks, she felt Bristol calling her.

The last customer had left the café, so she went into the shop to potter around. It was just after three, and the mid-afternoon lull had kicked in. With the sun shining, people were getting in their afternoon swim.

Feeling at the end of everything, Grace went outside

and sat down on one of the café's outdoor tables. She rubbed her temples, took a deep breath, tried to calm down. It would be all right in the end, one way or another. Out over the beach, a seagull suddenly cried out, followed by a shout of 'Bugger got my ice-cream!'

Grace smiled. Things could always be worse.

A couple of people were heading towards the shop. Grace stood up, about to head back inside, when a little whimper came from behind her. She stood up and walked over to the shop front to investigate.

Standing between a rack of polystyrene surfboards and a stack of buckets, as though using them for protection, was a little boy.

He had fair hair and blue eyes filled with tears. He couldn't have been more than five or six. His brightly coloured Toy Story swimming shorts were still wet from the sea, and he had a towel dusted with sand wrapped around his shoulders.

'Are you all right?' Grace asked, squatting down in front of him. 'What's your name?'

'Ben,' he whimpered. 'Where's Mummy? I can't find Mummy.'

'You're lost?'

Grace looked around. The promenade was nearly empty, most people on the beach. At the far end, Joan was sitting on a bench beside Jason, the chips on the seat of her wheelchair in front of them. Grace gave them a frantic wave. When Jason pointed, she waved for them to come back.

'We'll find your mummy,' Grace said. 'Let's get you an ice-cream and we'll sit you down until your mummy gets here.'

She led the little boy into the shop, and had him point out an ice-cream flavour. To her amusement he chose honeycomb. Grace scooped him out a child-size portion, then for good measure stuck a fudge stick in the top. Then, she led him outside to the tables and waited for Joan and Jason to make their way across the street.

'Get the word out,' Grace said. 'This is Ben. He's lost his mum.'

Jason nodded. 'On it.' He started running back up the promenade in the direction of the beach and the lifeguard hut.

'Go and check the pub,' Joan said. 'His mum might be in the family room. I'll stay here with Ben.'

'Can I have a ride in your car?'

Joan grimaced. 'It's a chair, but, ah, sure.' Glancing at Grace, she said, 'Hurry up.'

Grace ran for the Low Anchor. As she reached the main doors, she felt a little uneasy. She hoped one of the staff was on, but what if it was Daniel? She wasn't sure if she could face him. Taking a deep breath, she closed her eyes, then pushed inside.

The pub had that mid-afternoon lethargic feel. A couple of kids in sandals were playing darts, while a group of old ladies sat drinking coffees by the window overlooking the beach.

Both Daniel and Isabella stood behind the bar, standing close to each other, talking quietly. They looked like a perfect couple, and for a moment Grace felt the familiar pang of regret. Then she remembered her mission.

'Hi, Grace,' Dan said, noticing her as he looked up. 'All right?'

'Dan, sorry. We've got a lost kid. His name's Ben. Can you ask around?'

'Really? Oh, sure. There were a couple of families in earlier. I'll go and ask in the other bar.'

'Is he all right?' Isabella asked as Daniel went through a door behind the counter.

'I think so. Hopefully we'll find his mother in a minute.'

Glancing through the windows at the beach, she saw Jason standing outside the lifeguard hut.

'No luck,' Daniel said. 'We're not busy, though. Me and Izzy will come and help you look.'

'That would be great.'

'Ben, wasn't it?'

'That's right.'

'Got it.'

Grace headed back outside. Over on the beach, the speakers from the lifeguard hut were relaying the information, but facing the beach, it was impossible to hear clearly for anyone in the streets behind the promenade. Grace ran down the steps from the pub, cupped her hands around her mouth and began shouting out for Ben's mother. Behind her, she heard Daniel and Isabella doing the same.

Joan was still outside the shop with Ben, now playing a game of Connect Four with the little boy, a couple of bags of crisps open on the table. Grace ran past them into the narrow streets back from the promenade and called out again.

She had gone no more than a couple of doors when a woman in her mid-thirties, wearing a wide-brimmed sunhat and sunglasses, came running out of a little souvenir shop.

'Ben?'

Grace waved and she came running over. 'Are you Ben's mother? He's fine, don't worry. We've got him over at the shop.'

'Oh, thank heavens. I turned around for just a moment—'

She started to cry. Grace put an arm around her and led her back to the shop. Ben jumped up at the sight of her and ran into her arms.

'Ben, there you are!' the woman said, pulling her sunglasses off and tossing them aside as she scooped the boy off the ground and hugged him close. 'What did you have to go wandering off for?'

Joan looked up at Grace and sighed. 'Nice one,' she said. 'Kid's a gun at Connect Four too. Beat me three times in a row. I was really trying, as well.'

Daniel and Isabella had reappeared, and a few other locals who had belatedly joined the search had also gathered around. Grace waved, and over by the lifeguard hut, Jason gave them a thumbs up.

'Thank you so much for looking after him,' the woman said, hugging the boy to her. 'That's a mother's nightmare. I'm so glad you were looking out for him.'

Grace smiled. 'We're just happy to help.'

'This is such a lovely place,' the woman said. 'Everyone's so friendly. Really, I mean it. I'm so glad we came here rather than going abroad.'

'Stop by anytime,' Grace said. Squatting down in front of Ben, she said, 'If you promise to stay near your mum, you can have another ice-cream.'

'Can I play games with the car lady?' he said, pointing to Joan. 'She's not very good.'

Grace smiled as Joan rolled her eyes. 'Any time you like.'

Jason came running over with one of the lifeguards. As people asked after Ben, Joan turned and lifted her hands.

'Ice-creams for everyone!' she shouted.

A couple of minutes later, with everyone standing around outside with ice-creams in their hands, talking and laughing in small groups now that the tension of the search was over, Ben's mother asked if she could take a photograph. She balanced her camera on the bottom of an upturned bucket, then everyone gathered around, holding up their ice-creams.

'Would it be okay if I posted it on Instagram?' she asked, looking down at her camera's screen a few moments later. 'It's come out so well.'

Most people shrugged or nodded. Joan started to laugh. 'If you really want,' she said. 'Make sure you give us a tag. I think we have about ten followers.'

'Eleven,' Jason said. 'I followed you with the Surf Shack's account yesterday.'

'And that's why you're so wonderful,' Joan said.

'Doing my best.'

As the woman led Ben away, Daniel wandered over to where Grace stood at the edge of the patio.

'Good work,' he said.

'Thanks.'

'I imagine you get used to these dramas when you live in the big city.'

'It's a minefield,' Grace said.

'Come up for a beer sometime,' Daniel said. 'We've not really caught up since you got back. I'd love for you to get to know Isabella and the kids.'

Grace smiled. 'Sure.'

As Daniel wandered away, Grace caught a look from Joan. She pouted back, raising her eyebrows. Joan frowned, shaking her head, giving Grace a quizzical look. Grace just smiled.

As she headed into the café, she realised something. For the first time since her return, she'd been able to hold a conversation with Daniel that felt natural. No butterflies, no awkward silences, no uncomfortable concern about whether she was standing too close or too far away. No broken sentences or trying to talk at the same time, and no aching hole in her heart as he walked away.

'Huh,' she muttered, shaking her head.

It seemed she was finally over him.

31

DATE NIGHT

Paul had dressed up for the occasion. Grace, feeling a little casual in a summer dress and sandals, smiled as he held out a small bag.

'What's this?'

'Just a little gift.'

She lifted the flap of the bag and peered inside. A star-shaped cactus, a single flower blooming on the top.

'Um, thanks.'

'I figured if you had a rubbish time, you could just put it on my car seat or something, save you having to slash my tires.'

'I see.' Grace smiled. 'Now that you've charmed me with the gift, where are you going to take me for dinner? Haddock Enough Yet?'

'I would but it's closed on Tuesdays. I did try to reserve the two plastic seats by the counter for next Thursday, in case we made it to a second date, but the owner told me they're exclusively for drunks.'

'A shame.'

'I was heartbroken.'

'So you were already thinking about a second date?'

Paul shrugged. 'I figured you'd be so disappointed by tonight that you'd want to punish me by making me go through it all again.'

'Who says I'm going to be disappointed?'

'It depends how windy it is.'

'Really? So where are we going?'

Paul smiled. 'I figured everywhere would be crowded with tourists, so I decided we'd have a picnic.'

'Really?'

'I made sandwiches.'

'Oh?'

'And I baked a cake.'

'A cake?'

Paul smiled. 'A cheesecake. With honeycomb in it.'

'Uh, honeycomb?'

'That crumbly stuff you get in the baking section of Tesco.'

Grace just nodded. She wasn't sure whether to be stunned more by the obvious clue to his secret identity, or that he'd prepared them food.

'Are you ready?'

'Uh, yeah.'

Paul drove them down Melrose Hill and turned on to the road leading out to the cliffs above Sharker's Rock.

'Don't worry,' he said, as they crested the hill. 'I have it on good authority that the weather will clear up. We'll get a beautiful sunset, and it's a full moon tonight.'

'Are you good at reading the weather?'

Paul shook his head. 'But I know someone who is.

Someone who spends half his life staring at tide tables and weather reports.'

Another hint. Grace wasn't sure whether to be excited or disappointed. Part of her was thrilled that she was on a date with the Masked Surfer, but another part was growing to quite like Paul just as Paul. He had a quirkiness to his personality which gave her a warm feeling inside.

Paul stopped the car in a little car park on the cliff top. He switched off the engine, then peered up at the sky. He grimaced, then looked at his watch, before turning to Grace.

'I think we'd better take torches, just in case.'

'And raincoats?'

'Yeah, maybe.'

'Are you going to tell me where we're going yet?'

Paul grinned. 'I know a good spot.'

'Joan knows I'm on a date with you,' Grace said. 'So don't think about turning into a werewolf or anything like that.'

Paul nodded at the bag. 'You'd better bring that cactus just in case you need to fight me off. Ah—' He looked at his watch as the world outside suddenly brightened, the evening sun breaking through the clouds, banishing them away to stand proudly above the horizon in all its evening splendour. 'Right on time.'

They got out of the car. Grace looked up, stunned. The gloom that had hung over Blue Sands all day had gone. Low above the village, a full moon had just appeared in the sky.

'Are you ready?' Paul asked. 'We'd better hurry or the curry will get cold.'

'The curry?'

'Yeah. I like a bit of spice.'

Paul lifted the straps of two heavy coolers over his

shoulders, despite Grace's offer to help. She was quietly impressed by his obvious strength, even if she insisted on carrying a light bag filled with plastic cutlery. With Paul leading, they headed off down the path. From the car park it followed the line of a field downhill in the direction of Sharker's Rock, but halfway there, Paul stopped by a gateway leading to a higher field and put the coolers down. With a conspiratorial grin, he turned to Grace.

'This is the bit you have to promise not to tell about,' he said, nodding at the field beyond the gateway. 'This is private property, and the farmer gets a bit salty about people on his land. Absolutely no litter and ideally no footprints, otherwise there'll be a moaning article in the village rag next month.'

Grace smiled. 'I'll do my best. Where are we heading?'

'Up the hill. To the old lighthouse.'

'The lighthouse? We're on the wrong side of the bay.'

'Not that lighthouse. The other one.'

'There's another one?'

Paul grinned. 'It's not so well known, but I suppose that's one of the quirks of working in the village museum. You have to know these things for when some old guy comes in armed with printouts from the internet.'

'I had no idea there was another lighthouse in Blue Sands.'

'Well, there's not a lot left of it.'

He helped her over the gate, then passed over the coolers. Together, they started up the hill. The field was the highest point near the village, with a stand of rugged, wind-hassled trees at the top. Paul, though, led them past the trees and through a side gate into another field which sloped down towards Sharker's Rock, giving her a view of Blue Sands she had never seen before, the whole bay curving out below her, lights flicking on as the last rays of sunlight outlined the horizon. And from here, they were high enough just to see the lights of village on the top of the hill.

'Can you see that light right on the edge there?' Paul said, pointing. 'The green one? That's where I work. I put a filter over it just to see if I could see it or not. I'm not actually supposed to leave it on.'

'The whole village looks amazing,' Grace said. 'I had no idea you could see it from this angle.'

Paul touched her arm, and nodded to a concrete square below them. A stone plaque stood nearby, and there was a wooden bench set back on a little gravel area, sheltered by the hedge from the breeze drifting up the hill from the sea.

'Our restaurant,' Paul said, somehow managing to pick up both coolers with one arm while offering Grace his other. 'Shall we?'

'My pleasure,' Grace said, taking his arm, glad it wasn't too far. 'Is this it? The old lighthouse?'

As they reached the patch of concrete, Grace shone her torch on the plaque, illuminating a carved picture of a pretty lighthouse and a few paragraphs of information.

'This is all that's left,' Paul said. 'It ceased operation around nineteen fifty and was abandoned. There wasn't considered a need for two lighthouses so close together, and this one cost more to run and maintain. Much of the stone was removed and used in local buildings. We're actually on National Trust land—hence the plaque and the bench—but old Mr. Webber who owns the neighbouring field is in a dispute with the council over access. His argument is that too many people leave the gate open, which is why he's put up NO ENTRY signs everywhere and shouts at people trying to visit the site.'

'That's not very nice.'

'I offered him a free lifetime pass to the museum and library,' Paul said. 'But he wasn't interested.'

'Um, isn't entry free?'

Paul grinned. 'Yeah, it was kind of a joke. He didn't laugh.'

'I bet he didn't.'

'I offered him a free parking space if he didn't want to pay for parking down at the beach.'

'I bet that didn't go down well either.'

Paul shrugged. 'How was I supposed to know his farm was actually closer?'

They began to set out the picnic. Paul produced a battery-powered electric blanket out of a rucksack and laid it down over the concrete. At Grace's quizzical expression, he just shrugged and said, 'Got it on the internet.'

It turned out that Paul was an excellent cook, and had clearly spent some hours preparing the food. Everything was home-cooked, from sandwiches to curry-filled pastries, even a cheesecake which he grumbled had 'sunk a bit in the middle,' but tasted amazing. There was enough food for about six people, and even though Paul muttered about how he'd put too much salt in this or not enough mayonnaise on that, Grace eventually got him to confess that he'd studied catering at college and that cooking was still his main hobby, even if he only really cooked at home.

That Paul hadn't ballooned into some beach ball with such skill at his fingertips defied belief, but Grace figured that was why he hit the waves at secretive times of the day and night. However, she still couldn't figure out why.

All the food gave her another idea, though.

'I don't suppose—if Joan was interested—you'd work in the café a couple of days a week? Specifically doing food?'

Paul shrugged. 'I don't know. Maybe.'

'We're in a bit of a competition with a certain other café.'

'Is that so? Well, I'll think about it. I prefer to cook for my friends and family, though. It takes the pressure off.'

'Well, if....'

She trailed off. Paul was staring over her shoulder, shaking his head. 'I don't believe it,' he said. 'He's out of his mind. It must be nearly ten o'clock. It'll be dark soon.'

Grace turned to look down at the bay, and her heart sank. A man was paddling out across the water on a surfboard, heading for Sharker's Rock. She had no doubt it was the Masked Surfer, even though at this distance and in the failing light he was just a blur of movement against the water.

'Is that the secret guy?' Grace said, her throat suddenly dry, every word feeling like an awkward challenge just to flip it off her tongue.

Paul chuckled. 'Yeah, I suppose it is.'

'Oh.'

There must have been something in the way she spoke, because Paul suddenly turned towards her, a frown on his face. 'Grace? You didn't ... think it was me, did you?'

'Ah....'

Paul looked momentarily crestfallen. 'I don't know how to surf,' he said quietly, turning away.

'It's okay, I just—'

'Don't worry about it. Is that the only reason you agreed to come on a date with me?'

Grace gave a frantic shake of her head. 'No, I mean, yes, I did think it was you, but that's not the only reason I—'

'It's okay.'

'No, really, I'm actually glad he's not you, because I kind of like you the way you are, and—'

'It's fine. I mean it.'

Paul still couldn't meet her eyes. She was certain that she had blown it, and only in the moment of utter failure did she realise that she actually really liked Paul, that she had been having a great time, and it didn't really matter whether he was the Masked Surfer or not. In fact, she liked that he was who he was without hiding behind a secret identity, because if he was the person who had prepared such a wonderful picnic and taken her to such a beautiful spot, then really everything was already right about him—

'Can you keep a secret?' Paul said, looking up, a little twinkle in his eyes.

'What?'

'Out of interest, why did you think it was me?'

'Ah, well, he has your kind of build, and the same jaw, and you both like honeycomb ice-cream.'

Paul laughed. 'Everyone likes honeycomb ice-cream,' he said. 'It's the best flavour.'

'We sell more vanilla.'

'Ah, that's your stock ice-cream, though. That's for all the people too scared to be exotic. The type of people who've only ever had ice-cream out of the freezer at Morrison's. Once they've tasted honeycomb, there's no going back. Even butterscotch can't hold a candle.'

'It's still pretty good.'

'If you're going for a double-scoop, then it would be right to pair honeycomb and butterscotch, but you'd probably want the honeycomb on first, so that you eat the butterscotch first. Do you do doubles in the shop?'

'Not unless someone asks.'

'You totally should.'

'I'll mention it to Joan.'

The whole thread of their conversation had twisted. Down near Sharker's Rock, the Masked Surfer paddled into a roller and came bursting out of the spray to execute a slick turn.

'He's pretty good, isn't he?' Paul said with a hint of respect. 'I was always such a letdown. I mean, I can't even swim.'

'You can't … what do you mean you were a letdown? You know who that is?'

Paul smiled. 'You were right on the jaw and the build, even the ice-cream. You were just wrong on the generation. That guy down there … that's my dad.'

32

INFLUENCE

'WHAT DO YOU MEAN YOU'RE NOT COMING BACK DOWN?' Joan said, frowning. 'Coach needs to give you a good bollocking for not trying hard enough, before we get stuck into a couple of yesterday's leftover pasties.'

Grace smiled. 'I'm going to ride on up to the library and have morning coffee with Paul.'

'Dressed like that?' Jason asked.

'I have a change of clothes in my bag.'

'But you'll be all sweaty,' Jason said. 'Is he into his sportswomen?'

'I have a towel.'

Joan looked at Jason and grinned. 'Look at her. She's completely smitten. That must have been one hell of a date. I mean, judging on what was in that doggy bag you gave me, he can really cook.'

'Tell him if he bakes up a few of those cheesecakes I'll flog them in the Shack,' Jason said. 'Half price with a lump of board wax.'

Grace laughed. 'I'm sure he'll be delighted to hear that.'

'Just don't be late for work,' Joan said. 'I've had fourteen people ring up this morning to make a booking for lunch. Fourteen different people. I have no idea what's going on.'

'I won't.'

Jason leaned on the handlebars of his bike. 'Right. One more time. Are you ready? Let's train.'

Grace had forced herself to wait the traditional three days between their date and seeing Paul again. When she had jokingly told him what she planned, he had shrugged and told her he would be waiting. Last night, when she had finally cracked and stood outside the Low Anchor to pick up a Wi-Fi signal, he had replied almost straight away that he would be waiting with breakfast.

The museum and library didn't officially open until ten o'clock, but when Grace arrived at seven-forty-five, parking her pink BMX against the wall outside, she found an arrow taped to the glass doors bidding her to go up the stairs. On the second floor, more arrows led her through the modest exhibits to the balcony terrace that had a view over the valley below.

Paul was standing beside the glass doors that opened onto the terrace.

'Good morning,' he said. 'You look … energised.'

'Thanks.'

'How was your time?'

Grace shrugged. 'Three seconds better than yesterday, but still fifteen seconds slower than Jason, and a whole minute slower than Mike Anderson. As long as someone beats him, I'll be happy.'

'Didn't you tell me you liked Mike Anderson? He was your spinning teacher or something?'

Grace scowled. 'I used to. He came in the shop the other day while I was out, then complained on social media about the size of the ice-creams.'

'Ooh, catty.'

'It's become something of a grudge match. The current plan is for me to get just enough ahead of him to put him off while Jason powers through for the win.'

'Isn't that cheating?'

'I prefer to consider it aggressive competing. However, the likelihood of either of us getting anywhere near him is remote. He was a spinning teacher for a reason.'

Paul smiled. 'I think you're amazing just for trying it. That bench halfway up Melrose Hill was put there just for people like me who can't even walk it in one go.'

All the tables on the terrace, bar one, had been moved aside. Paul had moved the last table to the edge of the balcony with one chair on either side. An elaborate breakfast setup had been arranged, with muffins sliced and placed in a silver holder, coffee in a filter jug, orange juice that looked freshly squeezed.

'This looks wonderful,' Grace said.

Paul smiled. 'Take a seat,' he said, pulling out a chair for Grace to sit down. 'Help yourself to everything while I get the main dish.'

'The main dish?'

'You have a choice of two. Would you like to know your options?'

'Sure.'

'Beans on toast, or beans to the side, in a bowl, with toast on the plate. All served with various bits and bobs, mushrooms, egg, sausage, all the usual.'

'Fantastic. I'll have the beans on the toast.'

'The best way, so that they mingle with the butter. Coming right up.'

'I didn't know you had a kitchen here.'

Paul shrugged. 'There's one hob and a microwave. You learn to make do. I'll be back in two minutes.'

'You're versatile, that's for sure.'

Paul shrugged. 'Still can't swim, though. Or surf.' He gave her a little smile that hinted at regret. 'Are you sure you're not disappointed?'

After Paul's revelation, which even a few days later left her stunned, she had expected to be. But it was shock more than anything else.

'No,' she said, shaking her head. 'I'm not.'

She waited for him to bring the beans on toast, which came with all the English breakfast trimmings and a sprig of parsley on the side which Paul said added a professional touch.

'So,' she said, when she had stopped laughing, 'the Masked Surfer is really your dad?'

Paul rolled his eyes. 'He was a junior regional champion,' he said. 'He ended up scaling it back as a hobby when he went into teaching, but since he landed the film role last year, he's taken it up again. Getting into character, he calls it, even though he doesn't actually have to do any surfing in the movie. He just wants to look the part but keep it all a big secret from his pupils until the movie comes out. That's Dad down to a T. He always was a poser.'

The story had seemed fanciful, but Grace had looked online for it and found Paul was right. A Cornish surfing movie titled Way of the Waves was set to begin filming in September. Paul's dad had landed the role of Ark, a grizzled loner who befriends a bullied kid. Together they bond over surfing, with Ark coaching the kid into an

Olympic hopeful while dealing with his own issues at the same time.

'Ark isn't a very Cornish name,' Grace said.

'Apparently it's short for Arkansas. The production company is Canadian. I think technically it's a black comedy, but Dad's treating it like a war movie. And the level of secrecy he's going to is hilarious. Mum had a fit when she found out he was renting a van just to go surfing, but he does it under an assumed name and everything.'

'I feel kind of weird. I sort of hit on him.'

Paul laughed. 'He mentioned that there was a beautiful surfer girl who had fluttered her eyelashes at him. He was made up about it. And then he said he recognised you, and remembered a time when you had been sick in drama class. He said it was a real test of his acting to keep a straight face.'

'He remembers that? Oh my god.'

'He brings it up every time I mention you.'

Grace wasn't sure whether to be more surprised about Paul talking about her to his parents or that his dad remembered the one time she had been sick in class, when the day's assignment had been to express shock at the tragic passing of a beloved pet. Grace had gone a bit over the top, if she remembered rightly.

'It was only a bit of bile.'

'It stained the carpet.'

'It did not.'

Paul shrugged. 'He said it did. He's a teacher. Aren't we supposed to believe them?'

Grace was about to reply when her phone buzzed. She looked up at Paul, who just nodded. 'Enjoy your signal while you can,' he said.

It was Joan. Grace put the call onto speakerphone. 'Are you all right?'

'Are you still having breakfast with cookery boy? Can you hurry up? I've had nineteen people ring up this morning wanting a booking. I have no idea what's going on, but I think we're going to be busy. I managed to get hold of Hedges in time to double the pasty order, but is there any chance master chef can come down and help out?'

Grace cringed, but Paul just smiled. 'Hi, Joan,' he said. 'I'll close the library for lunch at eleven and come down to help.'

'Oh, you're still there? Um, hi, Paul. Thanks.'

As Grace ended the call, Paul frowned. 'Why so busy?' he asked. 'Is there some kind of special event on?'

Grace nodded at her phone. 'While I have a signal, do you mind if I take a look?'

'Not at all.'

It only took her a minute to figure it out. She held up her phone for Paul to see, shaking her head in disbelief.

'That lady the other day, the one whose boy wandered off, I thought she looked familiar. Turns out she's an Instagram influencer.'

Paul laughed. 'Really? Isn't everyone these days? How many followers does she have?'

'Three point four million. Oh, wow. And she posted that picture of us outside the café, and linked it to Google Maps, quoting it as the friendliest café in Cornwall. Who'd have thought it?'

'I guess I'd better go and find a clean apron.'

Grace stared at the picture. The woman had put it through a filter, turning it into a line drawing of a group of people with their arms around each other's shoulders, the beach and the cliffs in the background. It was a bit busy, but with a few adjustments....

'I have to go,' she said, standing up. 'Seriously, that was

the best breakfast I've ever had, and you can make it for me whenever you like, but I have something I really need to do on the way back to the café. I'm sorry.'

Paul just laughed. 'It's all good. Don't tell me, you have to see a man about a dog?'

'Close. A woman about a t-shirt.'

33

HOBBIES

Joan had tears in her eyes as she held up the plastic-wrapped t-shirt she had just taken from a box. 'Oh, Grace. It looks wonderful. I'm not quite sure what I'll say to Mum about changing the café's name, but I suppose that's a relatively minor issue.'

'You need to convince her to stay open first. The rest is easy.'

Joan was shaking her head. 'I'd call you a genius, but I saw the monstrosities you came up with before this one, so it's better just to call you persistent. This, though ... this is perfect.'

Sky blue, it had a group of characters with their arms around each others' shoulders. Grace had asked Mrs. Oldfield to base her design on the photograph, with a couple of extras thrown in. One character was a surfer, another in a wheelchair. At the front were a young boy and girl, behind them an older couple who could be parents. On the opposite side, Grace had requested a dog be added for good measure.

Behind the group was an image of the beach, the cliffs

on either side, and the sun setting over the horizon. Underneath, in bold lettering: Blue Sands Friendship Café.

The door pinged and Hedges came striding in, pushing a stack of pasty boxes. As he set the trolley down, he noticed the t-shirt.

'Good morning, girls. Nice threads. Upping the stakes?'

'You like it?'

'Can I order a set for the family? We'll wear them at the gala next weekend. Time to pick sides, isn't it? You think Jason has the mettle to pull it off?'

Joan laughed. 'He's out there now, doing extra laps. He's not giving up, that's for sure.'

Hedges nodded. 'Get him in one of those t-shirts and the extra drive will do it. Any chance of a honeycomb ice-cream for the road?'

'Did you bring us that extra order?'

'In the van.'

'Then you have a deal.'

'Nice one.'

Hedges unloaded the pasties and headed back out to the van for more. Grace turned to Joan. 'How many bookings have we got today?'

Joan sighed. 'Forty-three. It's insane. And since you got Paul to come down at lunchtimes, they've been rebooking. Our online reviews are through the roof. I don't know how you managed it, Graceful. I saw Sophie outside on the way down from Melrose Hill, and she practically put a curse on me. I mean, I know it's a barbeque pit she has out on the patio up there, but it looks like a cauldron. I'd swear there was something green swirling around in there.'

'It was just luck,' Grace said.

'Not a chance. *You're* luck,' Joan said. 'Lucky for all of us.'

'Is it still cool to have the afternoon off?'

Joan nodded. 'No problem. Mum's hired a couple more kids to help out. We're good. The surf's going to be flat, though. You'd be better getting a bus down to Newquay if you need to practice for the comp.'

Grace shook her head. 'I want to teach Paul to swim,' she said.

Joan's smile dropped. 'Teach … Paul? Then, he's not…?'

Grace gave a disappointed shake of her head. 'I'm afraid not. He does know who he is, though. He said I could tell you if I swore you to secrecy.'

Joan glared at Grace. 'You mean, you have a secret and you didn't immediately tell me, your best friend? What's going on?'

'It's a really big secret.'

'In that case, I forgive you. Make me a coffee—two sugars—and spill.'

'No … way.' Joan shook her head. 'Paul's making that up, surely. I mean, he works in a museum and library, he's surrounded by fantasy and he has nothing to fill his idle mind. He must be making it all up.'

'Apparently not. I thought it was pretty mad, too.'

'You need proof. I won't believe you without proof.'

'Well, he wants me to meet his parents, so I guess I can just ask straight out.' Grace shrugged. 'I'll get really drunk, then lean on his dad's shoulder and say, "Excuse me, are you the Masked Surfer who I hit on the other week?" I reckon that'll go down great.'

'Don't forget, this is still Mr. Davis, our old drama teacher.' Joan suddenly slapped Grace's knee and gasped. 'Oh my god. Paul wants you to meet his parents?'

'I suppose I'd only be meeting his mum for the first time, having previously been sick on his dad's classroom carpet.'

'Oh, I remember that. It was pumping out. It was round school for weeks that they didn't serve pumpkin soup at school because you ate it all.'

'What are you talking about? I don't remember that.'

'I did my best to shield you.'

Grace scowled. 'I don't know whether to be heartbroken or thankful.'

Joan ignored her. 'You have to meet his parents? That's like, next stage.'

'Have you met Jason's?'

Joan rolled her eyes. 'We have dinner every Wednesday night. It's like a family tradition. But, oh man, they're such nerds. It's like Jason came out the other side, but they're still stuck in this geek world. Last week his dad wanted to show me his train set. I thought it would be some big posh thing in the cellar, but no, it was in a box, and we had to clip it together and everything. Then he was like, which locomotive do you want? He said 'locomotive', not 'train'. Who calls them that, apart from train workers and anoraks?'

'Which one did you choose?'

'A blue one called Bessie. I derailed it on the first turn. You can get some real speed going if you double press the joypad button. His dad got annoyed because this bit fell off. I felt guilty, but not so much.'

'I'm glad you're so happy.'

'Don't mock me. If Paul isn't the Masked Surfer, how'd he get such ripped shoulders? I bet it's from lifting boxes of Games Workshop magazines. Or his collection of stamps.'

'Shut up. I'll ask him later.'

'A quid says he's into Dungeons & Dragons.'

'All right.'

'You might as well pay up now.'

Grace smiled. 'We'll see.'

Paul proved to be a false beginner when it came to swimming, although his progress from water-phobia to basic competence wasn't without its pitfalls. At his first lesson, Grace made him swim in beach shorts because he showed up in Speedos left over from school. And much as she wanted to see what was under the black t-shirt he had brought, he had forgotten to apply any suntan lotion to his fair skin on what was the hottest day of the summer so far, so the session looked like life-saving training as Paul, fully clothed, flapped and thrashed his way through waist-deep water, all with a wide grin on his face, as though he couldn't be happier.

At their second lesson, the following day, Paul showed up in a pair of trunks and a swimming t-shirt from J's Surf Shack. As they thrashed about in the water, Grace noticed the swell getting up. Paul, full of confidence, began to body-surf, while Grace stood and watched with exasperation, wondering if he was really as inept as he had claimed.

She was standing in the shore break, watching Paul's floundering legs, when a voice said, 'Hey.'

Daniel, behind her, was pushing his board out into the surf. He smiled as she noticed him, then nodded out into the waves.

'Only a couple of days until the gala,' he said. 'I heard you're in the surfing competition. This might be your last chance to practice. What are you doing, anyway?'

Grace gave an awkward shrug. Daniel hadn't noticed Paul, but now he came wading out to meet them.

'Hey, Dan.'

'All right, Paul?'

Grace tried to detect a terseness between them, a note of rivalry, but there was nothing. If not friends, they seemed like amicable acquaintances.

'Good, you?'

'Not often we see you in the sea.'

Paul smiled. 'Grace is being kind enough to teach me to swim.'

Dan pouted. 'Is that so? About time you learned. Are we going to see you on a board sometime soon?'

Paul shook his head. 'Probably not. We'll see.'

'Well, have a good one. I need to get out to those sets before they blow out. Take it easy. See you later, Grace.'

As Daniel paddled off into the surf, Grace stared at the water, a ragged mess of thoughts running through her mind.

'Are you all right?'

Grace looked up. Paul was watching her with a smile on his face.

'Huh? Yeah, I'm fine.'

'If you want to quit for the day, I'm happy for you to go out and get some waves. I've got something I wanted to do this afternoon, anyway.'

'No, it's cool, I just feel a little weird.'

Paul laughed. 'The old boyfriend meets the new boyfriend kind of thing?'

Grace looked up. 'Are you my boyfriend now?'

Paul just shrugged. 'If you want me to be.'

A little breaker suddenly struck her, soaking her up to the neck in froth and spray. Despite the shock of the water, Grace felt a tingle of warmth across her skin.

'Yes,' she said, meeting Paul's eyes. 'I do.'

His smile was kind and easygoing. 'Great, then we're still on for tomorrow? It's my turn to teach you something.'

The sun was just setting over the sea. From a viewing spot along the path out to Sharker's Rock, Joan lifted her glass of wine and turned to Grace.

'To you and me, best friends.'

Grace smiled and lifted her own glass. 'Best friends.'

They drank. Out across the sea, ripples of orange and red flickered in the dying light. A few seagulls glided across the water. Down by the shoreline, a couple of kids were throwing rocks into the sea, while from the promenade, the soft sound of music drifted over to them.

'Mum loved the design,' Joan said. 'She said she's going to call the sign people next week, then register with the council for a change of business name. "The Blue Sands Friendship Café". It sounds great, doesn't it?'

'Then she's not selling?'

Joan shook her head. 'Once she found out Sophie planned to turn it into a car park for Gourmet Garden customers, she was dead against it. Obviously, the sudden mass of extra business has helped too. They're still planning to move, though, so guess who's the new manager?'

'Congratulations.'

'I'll need staff, particularly if we get the year-round license I'm planning to apply for. No way I can spend all winter playing trains with Jason's dad. Are you interested?'

'In playing trains with Jason's dad? I suppose it depends which locomotive he lets me use.'

Joan rolled her eyes. 'In joining the team. I'm prepared

to make you a full partner. I have to remind you, though, that winters here can be long and bleak.'

Grace laughed. 'I remember them from the first eighteen years of my life. We'd have to drink a lot of wine to make it to the other side.'

'I'll drink to that. So, what do you say?'

'Let me think about it. If I win the surfing competition on Saturday, I might have to spend my winters in Brazil to prepare for the next World Championships.'

'Oooh, superstar,' Joan said. 'Top up?'

Grace held out her glass. 'Last one. Paul's picking me up early tomorrow.'

'Where are you going?'

'He's taking me out somewhere. He told me to wear decent shoes.'

'I bet it's to a comic book convention.' Joan took a sip of wine. 'Or to an antique teapots market.'

'You're such a cynic. And so what if he's into comics or antiques? We all have different interests.'

Joan sighed. 'Look at you, you're just gone. Completely. Why don't you just get married and move into the library together?'

'Because he hasn't asked me yet.' Grace slapped herself on the cheeks. 'Oh my god, did I just say that?'

'You've been seeing him, what, two weeks?'

'Three.'

Joan laughed. 'You've probably passed the current national average for relationship length already. At five weeks, Jason and me are practically antiques.'

'Where does the time go? I'll be a grandmother before I know it. Oh, speak of the devil….'

Ethel Dottington was leading Gerald up the path. The pug, reluctant, was dragging at his leash as the old woman tugged him towards a patch of couch grass. From where Grace and Joan sat, the sun's glare would have been in Ethel's eyes, and she clearly hadn't seen them sitting on the verge a little higher up.

'Come on, Gerald,' she said, urging the dog forward. 'Let's empty out that back end.'

She leaned down and began to pat the dog on the butt. Gerald, clearly aware of what he was supposed to do, squatted down and began to defecate. Grace and Joan exchanged looks, both trying not to laugh.

'Good boy,' Ethel said. 'That's my pretty Gerry. Right, let's get back before we catch our death.'

For a moment, Grace thought the old woman meant to just leave the dog's mess behind, but then, with a deft strike, Ethel stuck out a foot, kicking the lump up and over the edge of the cliff, down on to the beach.

'Oh dear,' she muttered. 'A little sticky tonight.'

She pulled a tissue from her pocket, reached down and wiped her shoe, before tossing the tissue into the grass. Grace and Joan watched, speechless, as Ethel retreated back down the path, tugging a more freely moving Gerald along behind her.

'I can't believe she just did that,' Grace said. 'We should have filmed it.'

'We can still catch her and give her a warning. Well, you can. Go on.'

Maybe it was the wine talking, or maybe not, but Grace found herself on her feet, stumbling down the path in Ethel's wake. She reached the old woman just as the path opened out at the top of the beach.

'Excuse me,' she said. 'Can I have a word?'

Ethel turned. 'Yes?'

'I, um, saw you kick your dog's mess over the top of the cliff. Haven't you seen the signs?'

Ethel frowned. 'What are you talking about?' she repeated.

'I just watched you. You're supposed to take it home.'

Ethel stared at her. 'What are you talking about?'

'Your dog just took a dump in the grass, and you kicked it over the edge of the cliff. Sometimes kids sit down there.'

'It's a little dangerous to sit so close to the cliff, isn't it? I'd hope they have more sense—'

'You're still not allowed to do it.'

Ethel's eyes turned hard. 'Don't you lecture me, young lady. That's the problem with today's youth. You think you know everything—'

'I know you're not allowed to let your dog crap by the side of the cliff path and kick it over the edge of the cliff. It's disgusting.'

'It's a natural process. Nature returns to nature.'

'So you admit it.'

'I'm admitting nothing. But there's nothing wrong with letting your dog do his natural business as long as you don't leave it for someone to step in.'

'Do you do your natural business in public?'

'How dare you! I've a mind to call a constable. And look at you—hardly in a position to tell me what to do, are you? Haven't *you* seen the signs?'

Ethel pointed. Grace turned, looking past the wine glass still in her outstretched hand at the red sign by the side of the path, which read:

NO GLASS OR BOTTLES ON THE BEACH

'It's plastic,' she muttered.

'Why don't you drop it and we'll see?' Ethel said. 'Are you even old enough to drink?'

'Of course I am!'

'I meant mentally.' Ethel lifted a finger and turned it in a circle beside her forehead. 'And people tell me I'm cuckoo.'

'You—'

Something was pressing against Grace's ankle. She looked down to see Gerald with his butt pressed up against her, rubbing it back and forth.

'Oh my,' Ethel said. 'It looks like we need to get the wormer out again, don't we?' Then, looking up at Grace, she added, 'I do hate the Cornish water. And the pipes in those chalets … right out of Victorian times.'

Without another word, she tugged Gerald away from Grace's leg and headed off into the evening. Grace watched her go, feeling like a balloon slowly deflating. Then, with a sigh, she walked dejectedly back up to where Joan was waiting.

'Any luck?'

Grace shook her head. 'Busted.' She held up the glass. 'These are plastic, aren't they?'

'Yeah, but the bottle's not.'

'Oops.'

'Oh, Grace, you always were useless in an argument.'

Grace sighed again. 'And I think I have ringworm in my ankle.'

34

SUNDOWN

'DON'T WORRY: WHERE WE'RE GOING, A HANGOVER WILL be the last thing you worry about,' Paul said, as he steered them into traffic on the A30. 'But, if you need to stop really quick, give me as much warning as you can.'

'I'll live. I think. Where are we going, anyway?'

'You'll see. It's not far now.'

A short while later, they turned off the dual carriageway and into the country lanes. Paul drove at Sunday-driver speed, but even so, by the time they pulled up at a small car park next to a field, Grace was only just keeping her stomach down. The fresh air had never felt better as she staggered out of the car.

'Right, this way,' Paul said, taking a massive hold-all out of his car's boot and slinging it over his shoulder.

'What's that?'

'My gear.'

Grace looked at the stile beside the gateway and the path that led across a moorland field before dropping out of sight. For South Cornwall, they were in as remote an area as it was possible to get.

'Saws and butcher's knives?'

Paul shook his head. 'Ropes.'

'Should I be scared?'

He laughed. 'Not at all. Maybe next time. Come on, let's go.'

They headed across the field, following a path along a line of weather-beaten trees. A handful of dirty sheep and some moorland ponies wandered across the thick grass, among lumps of lichen-covered granite, for the most part ignoring Paul and Grace unless they got too close.

After a few minutes of gentle uphill walking, they reached a gate. On the other side there were more rocks, and the ground dipped sharply away, the path leading into a rocky quarry.

'Best climbing in South Cornwall,' Paul said. 'Don't worry, it's safe. All the routes here are approved for people with the proper gear.'

'Rock climbing?'

Paul grinned. 'There's nothing like it.'

'Are you out of your mind?'

'Don't worry. I'm a certified instructor.'

Grace wondered what Joan would think. It explained the muscles she had seen through Paul's t-shirt at their swimming sessions. She wondered how they would feel under her hands, but the thought of moving their relationship on to the next stage was tempered as Paul pointed at a sheer rock face rising some fifty feet off the ground.

'On the American points system, that's a five point eleven,' he said, walking forward. 'Known here in the U.K. as very hard. We'll build you up to that one.'

'What am I starting on?'

He grinned. 'Over here. A five point eight. A beginner climb.'

He led her through the quarry to a lump of rock rising at a gradual angle to about ten feet.

'I could do that with my bare hands.'

'You've got to start somewhere.' He dropped the bag on the ground. 'Are you ready? I'll show you how it goes.'

Joan, stuffed a lump of caramel shortcake into her mouth and shook her head. 'Not fair. I want a library nerd boyfriend.'

'You've got one!'

'Ha, I forgot. Just think about all those other weeds at school who used to get ribbed all the time. They're probably all firemen and bodybuilders and pro-cyclists now.'

'Probably. Even Hedges is ripped from carrying all those pasties. And according to Becky, he's a stallion.'

Joan put up a hand. 'Please, please don't talk about Hedges. So, did Paul make you go freestyle up the hard bit? Bag of chalk and all that?'

'No! He was a perfect teacher. He showed me how it all worked, then helped me do it. Damn, my arms are killing me now.'

'Was that wise, with the gala's surfing competition tomorrow?'

'Probably not, but I was trying to impress Paul.'

'I don't think you need to impress Paul. I think you impress him enough just being you. Has he kissed you yet?'

'Shut up!'

'Has he? Come on, Grace. What's he waiting for?'

'We had a little … peck.'

'In the quarry? Was it all misty and windswept? Was he wearing a vest?'

'Look, just shut—'

The bell tinkled as the door opened. Ethel Dottington marched inside, holding up a dog's water bowl.

'Excuse me? There was a fly in the dog's water. Is that what you think about your customers' pets?'

Joan stared at her. 'I can't see a fly.'

'That's because I tipped it out.'

'I'll fill it up again,' Grace said, moving around the counter. 'Sorry about that.'

'Thank you,' Ethel said tersely. 'I trust you're sober this time?'

'I—'

'Not very professional, is it, drinking on duty?'

'We're not—'

'You can tell that to the council when they come to do an inspection,' Ethel said, then threw her hands up in the air and marched out, Gerald stumbling behind her. A little patch of yellow water stood near where he had been standing.

'Oh, that woman,' Joan said.

'I think he's drunk enough already,' Grace said, pointing at the pool of urine. 'I'll get a cloth.'

She had just made it back behind the counter when the door opened again, and this time a group of school kids came running in. Grace had barely lifted a hand before they had trampled the urine all over the shop floor. Grace looked at Joan. She couldn't help but smile.

'Oh, that woman,' she said.

~

The sun was beginning to dip. Grace looked up as Paul came walking across the road, carrying two pints of beer, and sat down beside her on the promenade wall.

'Isn't it lovely tonight?' she said. 'Not a cloud in the sky.'

Paul grinned. 'This is the moment where I'm supposed to say, "but not as lovely as you," isn't it?'

Grace rolled her eyes. 'I was being sarcastic. It's the last day of the gala tomorrow. The surfing competition. The sea's flat calm, so it won't be much of a competition if there's no surf.' She shrugged, then gently leaned against his shoulder. 'But, you know, if you want to say it, I won't be upset.'

'The day you came into the library was the most wonderful day of my life,' Paul said, waving a hand dramatically in the air. 'Filing thirty six volumes on British Wildflowers was driving me nuts, and then I looked up to see the most beautiful wildflower of all.'

Grace laughed. 'You saved it at the end there.'

'Thanks.'

'Do you really mean it? Not that it agrees with my semi-feminist stance on relationships, of course.'

'It's another way I disappointed my dad,' Paul said. 'I'm not one for acting. If I say it, I mean it.'

'I don't think you're a disappointment to him. I bet he thinks you're great.'

'He likes my cooking.'

'So do Joan's customers. She wants to offer you a job.'

Paul grimaced. 'I appreciate the offer, but … I'm not so into beaches. And in any case, my parents have applied to build a small café-restaurant next to the museum car park. Business picks up a lot in winter.'

'Really?'

'But I would be happy to do a bit here and there. Perhaps one or two days a week. Assuming you're still going to be here, of course.'

'I'm planning to be.'

'So you're not going back up to Bristol at the end of the summer?'

Grace frowned. 'I thought about it. A lot, actually. There are things I need to do if I'm going to stay here for longer. I can't stay in the chalet forever, so I'll need to find somewhere to live, but Joan's offered me a job, so we'll see.'

Paul put a hand over hers. 'I'd be happy if you stayed,' he said.

The sun had just begun to drop below the horizon. 'Now would be a good time for you to kiss me,' Grace said.

'Does your inner feminist agree?'

'It was my idea, so it's okay.'

Paul smiled. 'Good.'

35

COMPETITION

THE CAR PARKS WERE FULL, THE BEACH PACKED. WITH A bright sun shining overhead, the lightest of breezes, and beautiful rollers slicing the sea into neat curls—the result of some overnight Atlantic storm—hundreds of people had come for the gala. All along the promenade, shops, cafes and pubs had set up little stalls for the customers milling about. Sophie from the Gourmet Kitchen was selling French donuts that looked like regular donuts at twice the price, while Mike Anderson stood nearby, flexing his muscles while he signed autographed copies of a new book about biking in the Himalayas. Grace briefly attempted to talk to him, to see if he remembered her from spinning class, but as she got within earshot she heard some squealing fan asking him what he did to get his thighs so firm. Instead, she rolled her eyes and headed for the beach.

Paul unfortunately had to work in the morning, but promised he would try to make it down for the competition. Joan had roped Jason in to help with the Blue Sands Café's stall before he had to join the rest of the competition's judges, but Hedges' wife Becky had kindly offered to help.

'I'm just aching all over,' she was saying to Joan as Grace arrived, surfboard under her arm. 'I told him I had to help you out today, but when you're married to a man like that, you just want him to dominate you, don't you?' She squealed with delight before handing a vanilla ice-cream to a customer.

Joan, her face blank, stared at Grace. 'Help me,' she said.

'I'll be back soon with the trophy,' Grace said.

Joan winked. 'Go get the tro.'

Grace rolled her eyes. 'I would, but I think Daniel's got other ideas.'

Nearby, on the Low Anchor's temporary promenade bar, Daniel was waiting with his surfboard while Isabella gave him a shoulder massage. His two children were jumping up and down, shouting, 'Go, Dad! Go, Dad!'

'You'll be such a spoilsport if you beat him,' Joan said.

'I'm doing it for the café.'

'Good luck.'

A gong sounded from outside the lifeguard hut, and an amplified voice announced five minutes until the start of the competition, requesting all competitors and judges get to their positions.

'See you in an hour or so,' Grace said.

'If I'm still alive,' Joan answered, while beside her Becky began to do dramatic back stretches.

'Oh, he's such a titan between the sheets,' she said, laughing. 'I don't know how I got so lucky.'

Grace picked up her surfboard and headed over to the beach. She was nearly at the shoreline when Daniel called out to her.

'Hey, Grace,' he said, coming up beside her. 'Just like the old days, isn't it?'

She smiled. 'Only this time I'm not going to go easy on you. This time I'm going to kick your butt.'

He lifted an eyebrow. 'Is that a challenge?'

'It sure is.'

'Well, may the best person win.'

The announcer began to read out the names of the competitors in the mixed surfing competition. '...Rob Williams from Zennor, Brett James from Bude, Daniel Woakes from Blue Sands, Grace Clelland from Blue Sands, Eliza Wood from Penzance ... and Frank Davis from Blue Sands.'

At the mention of the last name, a ripple of surprise passed through the crowd. Grace turned to see Paul's dad, in full Masked Surfer gear, striding purposely down the beach. As he reached the rest of the assembled competitors, he reached up and pulled the mask over his head, revealing a grizzled version of the stern but entertaining teacher Grace remembered from school.

'No damn way,' Daniel said from behind her, as the now unmasked surfer smiled.

'May the best surfer win,' Frank said, in a voice which was clearly still in character for his upcoming movie. 'Might not be Sharker's Rock, but there's some blood to be taken out there, and some nature to be tamed.'

Daniel was sniggering. A couple of other local competitors were staring in disbelief. Grace smiled. 'Nice to meet you again, Paul's dad,' she said.

Frank Davis lifted an eyebrow. 'He's met a good one in you, lass,' he said. 'Doesn't mean I'm going to cut you any slack, though.'

'May the best surfer win.'

Frank Davis nodded. 'Indeed.'

'Into the water!' came a booming voice from the loud speaker. Frank Davis immediately broke into a run. Grace turned to follow, but Daniel was still laughing.

'Oh, that guy,' he said.

'Hurry up or you'll miss the start.'

The competition was a non-event. Every time Frank Davis paddled into a wave, roaring 'Mine!' at the same time, the rest of the competitors pulled back to watch as the old man cut and hacked his way across the surf like someone twenty years younger. From the start it was clear the battle was for second place, but Grace was proud of her performance, with a couple of solid rides, even pulling off a decent little flip on her final wave. As she carried her board back up the beach, however, she knew the best she could hope for was that she had beaten Daniel.

The competitors assembled outside the lifeguard hut for the announcement of the results. A crowd quickly gathered around them, clapping and cheering.

'You were awesome!'

Grace looked around. Joan gave her a wave as Becky pushed her chair over the gravel.

'We thought we'd better come over and commiserate with you,' Joan said. 'You were epic, but I don't think anyone was beating old Frank.'

'Who's looking after the café and the stall?' Grace asked, putting her board down on the rocks and giving Joan a wet high-five.

'Mum's in the shop, and we've got a special guest doing the ice-creams,' Joan said.

Grace looked across the beach to the promenade.

Wearing a chef's hat, Paul lifted a hand and gave her a thumbs' up.

'You really were awesome,' Joan said, shaking her head. 'Like you'd never been away.'

'As long as I beat Daniel I'll be happy.'

'Thank you everyone for coming,' came the announcer's voice over the loud speaker. 'What a great competition! Some wonderful surfing from locals, and from those from farther afield. And now … the judges' results are in. In third place … Brett James from Bude.'

'Wow, Daniel must have sucked,' Joan said, as Brett James gave a wave to claps and cheers from the crowd.

'And in second place … Daniel Woakes from Blue Sands.'

Grace turned to stare at Joan, who just shrugged. 'Perhaps Mr. Davis was only in it as a guest—'

'And in first place, with a performance that will long be remembered, the legendary Frank Davis from Blue Sands!'

A huge cheer went up from the crowd. To many backslaps, Frank Davis went to collect his trophy, shouting, 'Call me Ark!' as he went.

'What happened?' Joan asked, shaking her head. 'You were awesome.'

Grace just sighed. 'Oh, well. Not awesome enough.'

'Here's Jason,' Joan said, as Jason pushed through the crowd to meet them. He was frowning, his face etched with disappointment.

'So?' Joan said, as Jason gave a guilty grin. 'What happened? Grace was way better than that kid from Bude.'

Jason gave a sheepish grin. 'Yeah … turns out that wearing a J's Surf Shack wetsuit was a conflict of interest,' he said to Grace. 'You, um, got disqualified, and my results got nullified.' Then, with a cheerful pout, he added, 'If it makes you feel better, I had you in equal second place.'

'Equal?' Joan said.

'With that kid from Zennor,' Jason said. 'We went to the same surf school. He got disqualified as well.'

Grace could only laugh. 'Never mind,' she said. 'The best man won.'

On a makeshift podium made out of a picnic table carried down to the beach, Frank Davis was making a dramatic speech about the importance of education and physical fitness. He finished with a plug for his upcoming movie, then offered free surfing lessons to anyone willing to accompany him out to Sharker's Rock. Over on the promenade, Paul climbed up onto the wall and shouted, 'Go, Dad! You're a legend!'

'He's so embarrassing,' Joan said.

'Ah, it's sweet.'

'You're so gone. If you hadn't been disqualified you'd probably have lost anyway, because you were daydreaming about holding hands as you walked across the beach at sunset.'

'While eating honeycomb ice-creams.'

'Told you.'

'There's still the Melrose Hill Bicycle Race,' Jason said. 'You'll have to beat me and Mike Anderson, though.' He grinned. 'Good luck.'

'And Steve!' Becky shouted, clapping her hands together. 'He's been training in secret for months.'

'What?' Joan said, turning to Becky. 'Hedges—I mean Steve—has entered the bicycle race?'

'He needed somewhere to put his energy,' Becky gasped. 'There were only so many hours of sleep I could go without.'

Joan rolled her eyes at Grace. 'Becky, could you look after the stall until the start of the race? I want to give these two a pep talk.'

'Sure. I'll probably need a chair, because I'm still exhausted from last night.'

'If Jason will give me a piggyback, you can have mine.'

Becky laughed, but Grace grabbed the handles of Joan's chair and pushed her quickly away before she could make her offer serious. Jason trailed along behind them, occasionally pausing to turn and clap as Frank Davis's victory speech stretched over the ten-minute mark, with no sign of abatement.

Paul met them on the promenade and pulled a still-dripping wet Grace into a hug.

'You were fantastic,' he said. 'Yeah, I know Dad won, but you were still awesome.'

'I got disqualified,' she said. 'The wetsuit. I didn't realise the competition rules would be so strict, but I guess I was wrong.'

'Ah.'

'Becky's going to look after the stall,' Joan said. 'Come on, lover boy. We need to get these two match fit for the bicycle race.'

They headed back to Grace's chalet. Paul, Joan and Jason drank tea in the living room while Grace got changed out of her wetsuit and had a quick shower. Her arms were aching, and she felt sure she wouldn't even be able to walk up Melrose Hill, let alone ride. When she came into the living room, Joan was sitting next to Jason on the sofa, one hand on his shoulder, while Paul watched with an amused twinkle in his eyes.

'You keep Mike Anderson on the inside,' Joan was saying to Jason. 'If you have to, elbow him into the verge. No one complains about my café's ice-creams and gets away with it.'

'Isn't that cheating?' Grace asked.

'Oh, there you are. Doing your nails, were you?'

'I was washing away the scent of humiliation. You're not really expecting Jason to cheat, are you?'

Joan narrowed her eyes. 'It's not just about Jason, but about Blue Sands and the café,' she said. 'Do you really want Mike Anderson to win the race while wearing a t-shirt supporting the Gourmet Garden? It's not too late for Mum to change her mind.'

'No, but—'

'Then—' She frowned. 'What's that noise?'

They all fell silent. From somewhere nearby came a muffled cry of anguish, followed by the sound of little fists banging on a wall. Someone was expressing a level of misery unheard of in Blue Sands.

'Is that another lost kid?' Joan said, frowning.

As a screeched name came rattling through the walls, Grace shook her head.

'Nope. That's her next door.'

36

TO THE FINISH

'*GERALD!*'

'I'm gathering that the dog's dead,' Joan said, as Jason pushed her out onto the front path, behind Grace and Paul. 'Small mercies, I suppose—'

'*Gerald, where are you?*'

'Okay, maybe not.'

'Unless she's wondering what realm of heaven the dog's gone to,' Paul said.

'I knew you were into Dungeons & Dragons,' Joan said, making Paul laugh just as the door to Ethel's chalet flew open and the old woman stepped out, hair wild, still—bizarrely for three o'clock in the afternoon—in a dressing gown.

She took one look at them standing on the grass in front of Grace's chalet and bared her teeth.

'You did this,' she hissed. 'You took my Gerald. What have you done with my darling? I lie down for a short nap, and he's gone.'

'We haven't seen your dog,' Grace said, putting up a hand to silence a far more vicious comment threatening to come from Joan. 'We were relaxing before the bicycle race and we heard you crying.'

'He's gone,' Ethel said, her anger dissolving. She threw her hands up into the air then fell forward like a skydiver exiting a plane. Paul, displaying far better reactions than the rest of them, jumped over the partition fence and caught her inches above the cobblestone path. He lifted her up as though she were made of straw and sat her down on a bench beside the door.

'When did you last see him?' he asked.

'He went out into the garden for a little wander among the flowers, and I just lay down for a moment.'

'Then he might be round the back.'

'I just looked. He's gone.'

'Well, he can't have gone far. What kind of a dog is he?'

'A pug.'

Paul exchanged a glance with Grace. 'Um, well, pugs can't really do much more than waddle about, can they? How far can he possibly have gone? Don't worry, we'll find him.'

'He's a very active little thing. And when he sees a bird, he loses his mind a little bit.'

'We're going to miss the start of the race,' Joan hissed at Grace behind Jason's back. 'We have to go. Can we leave Paul to sort this out?'

Grace stared at Ethel as the old woman sobbed into her hands while Paul sat beside her, one arm around her shoulders, trying to offer comfort. Spiky and offensive she might be, but Ethel Dottington was still just an elderly lady, one who had lost her only friend.

Ignoring Joan, Grace said, 'We'll find him. Don't worry.'

She ran back through her chalet and out of the sliding

doors into the garden. She peered over the low fence at Ethel's garden, and quickly spotted a gap under the far side of the fence, big enough for a small dog to squeeze through. She ran back to the front and told the others.

'Come on,' she said. 'He can't have gone far.'

Joan, despite her protests, was left to sit with Ethel while Jason, Paul, and Grace checked the nearby streets. The little pug was nowhere to be seen. Grace was on the verge of giving up when a muted bark came from up ahead.

'Gerald!'

Hearing her shout, Paul and Jason came running over. Together they walked down a narrow alleyway between two rows of houses, following the sound of further barks. They emerged by a small river gushing down a stone-walled drainage channel through the centre of the village. To their right, it emerged from a culvert cut into the hillside, cascading down a little waterfall.

Gerald stood on the grass bank right above the culvert. He had got caught up in brambles and was struggling to get free. As they watched, he staggered a couple of steps, and one leg slipped, hanging out over the rushing water below. One more step and, brambles or not, he would fall in.

'The little mite'll drown if he goes in there,' Jason said.

Paul jumped into the river, the water splashing up to his knees and surging around him. He waded forward to the bottom of the culvert, but Gerald was just out of reach. Grace nodded at Jason, who crossed the river on a little footbridge and approached the grassy bank from the other side. Together, they climbed up, one step at a time, getting closer to Gerald while trying not to alarm him. The dog was whimpering nervously as he tried to tug himself free.

'Can you grab him, Paul?'

'Not yet. I can't quite reach him.'

'Jason, can you try poking him with a stick? See if you can knock him off into Paul's arms.'

Gerald, still caught in the brambles, gave a low, frustrated growl. Grace dug her feet into the grass and stretched her arms, trying to get a hold of him, but he was just out of reach. In the water below, Paul was moving back and forth, ready to catch him, while Jason, on the side where the brambles were thickest, was poking a stick through the thorns, trying to get the little dog to take a leap of faith.

'Come on, boy, don't be scared,' Grace said, trying to coax Gerald forward. The little dog grumbled again and started to turn, only for his back legs to slip over the edge. He gave a yelp as a bramble came loose, then he was scrabbling for safety.

'Quick, Jason, knock him off!'

Jason prodded the pug with the stick. He caught the little dog's feet, and Gerald dropped like a furry stone into Paul's arms. As Paul caught him, he fell backwards, splashing into the water, but even as his head briefly went under, he held the little dog aloft like a trophy while Grace and Jason cheered. Then, passing the dog to Grace, he climbed out, shaking himself off.

'God, it's freezing,' he said. 'And I thought the sea was cold.'

'Come on, quick, we can still make the race,' Grace said. At that exact moment, however, a distant horn blared, followed by a cheer. Grace glanced at Jason, who just shrugged.

'Mike Anderson had it in the bag anyway,' he said with a sheepish grin. 'Joan won't be best pleased, but it was inevitable really. Let's go get some ice-creams.'

With Grace carrying Gerald, they headed back to the chalets. Joan was sitting beside Ethel on the bench, the pair of them chatting amicably. At the sight of her dog, Ethel leapt up like a woman half her age, clapping her hands together with a soft thud.

'Oh, my Gerry! You're all right!'

Grace handed the dog over with relief. As Ethel showered the little pug with hugs, kisses, and promises of better future protection, Grace lifted an eyebrow at Joan.

'You have a new best friend, now, do you?'

Joan shrugged. 'Would you believe it, we bonded over cancer survival.'

'That's, um, nice.'

Joan's smile dropped. 'We missed the race.'

'It's all right. Neither me nor Jason really had a chance. I think we all knew that.'

'Why don't we take part anyway?' Paul said. He squeezed river water out of his t-shirt and grinned. 'It'll give me a chance to dry out a little bit.'

'My bike's at the Shack,' Jason said.

'And I left mine by the surf club. We can't join a bicycle race without wheels.'

'We have wheels.' Paul nodded at Joan's chair.

Joan looked around. 'And we have t-shirts. Come on. Let's go steel the Gourmet Kitchen's thunder.'

Ethel was still cooing over Gerald, but now she looked up. 'Thank you so much for saving my little baby,' she said. 'If there's anything I can do for you in return....'

Joan reached over and pulled a new t-shirt, still in its packet, out of the tray underneath her wheelchair. She held it up to Ethel.

'You can put this on,' she said. 'And you can come for a walk with us up Melrose Hill.'

'Oh, well, I don't think Gerald is up to the exercise right now—'

'He can sit on my lap,' Joan said. 'As long as he doesn't moult too much.'

At first none of the milling spectators noticed them, then, as people glanced back to see the line of sky-blue t-shirts, the wheelchair, the little dog, and even the old lady holding on to Grace's arm, people began to clap. By the time they were halfway up, the whole crowd was watching them, cheering as they passed. They overtook a couple of failed competitors sitting exhausted beside their bikes, each giving them a wave. Then, just a few metres from the top, they saw Mike Anderson, sitting beside the road, rubbing his left thigh while Sophie Baker stood over him.

'I told you we should have had an early night!' she snapped, wraithlike hair billowing around her as Mike Anderson flexed his leg and winced.

'Who won if he didn't?' Grace whispered to Joan, as they came over the brow of the hill, just in time to see a familiar figure step up onto a podium set up in the picnic area.

'And the winner of this year's Melrose Hill Bicycle Race, is … local boy, Steve—'

'Stallion!' screamed Becky, jumping up and down nearby.

'—Hedge!'

The crowd clapped and cheered as Hedges lifted a trophy over his head, then paused to wipe sweat out of one of his sideburns and blow Becky a kiss.

'Well, that's convenient,' Joan said, nodding at the sky-blue t-shirt Hedges wore, now dark in places with sweat. 'We're never going to hear the end of it, though.'

'Do you have anything to say?' the announcer said, going over to Hedges and holding out a microphone.

Hedges cleared his throat. 'This was a team effort,' he said. 'I'd like to thank my wife, Becky, my kids … and my fan club over there.'

As he pointed at Grace's group, the few members of the crowd who hadn't noticed them turned and began to clap. Jason waved and blew kisses to the crowd, Joan rolled her eyes, and Gerald gave a little grumble on Joan's lap. Ethel uttered an embarrassed laugh, while behind her back, Paul gave Grace's hand a little squeeze.

The promenade was abuzz with excitement. Grace and Joan had wondered who Becky had left in charge of their stall, but Becky had shrugged and simply said, 'Oh, some old guy. Kind of cool. Said he liked honeycomb ice-cream.'

To their surprise they had found Frank Davis surrounded by a group of wide-eyed kids, the ice-creams in their hands forgotten and melting as the old drama teacher and part time professional surfer regaled them with tales of freakish waves and daring surf moves. Paul rolled his eyes, peered into the ice-cream tubs inside the portable freezer, and shrugged.

'I think he was a little generous with his portions,' he said.

Joan looked at Grace. 'Barbeque at yours?'

Grace was about to reply when her phone, stuffed into a pocket of her shorts, began to buzz. She pulled it out, a couple of bars of the Low Anchor's Wif-Fi allowing an unknown number to get a connection. She answered, listening for a couple of minutes to the voice on the other end, then ended the call and looked at Joan.

'Huh. That was the police. Apparently I'm not going to prison. The charges against me got dropped.'

Joan clapped her hands together. 'Then we're breaking out the wine. The barbeque starts in half an hour.'

Grace looked at Ethel, who had accompanied them back down, partly because Gerald refused to leave Joan's lap.

'If Ethel doesn't mind.'

The old woman shrugged. 'It's been a long time since I had a decent piece of meat,' she said.

Grace grimaced. 'Ah, okay.'

'I have a new sea shanty,' Jason said, clicking his fingers and then beginning to clap in rhythm. 'Oh, he had a very good bike, all right, and he climbed Melrose Hill with all his might, but he was a sucker for a bit of fashion, and pulled his groin with a night of—'

'Wait until we're drunk,' Joan said, putting a hand on Jason's arm. She turned to Grace. 'Six o'clock at yours? Just give me an hour to sort this place out before Mr. Davis turns it into a pirate club.'

'And then the Kraken burst from the waves, knocking the old surfer to his knees!' Frank roared, arms aloft, as the assembled children gasped.

As Jason pushed Joan back across the promenade and Ethel, now back in possession of Gerald, stumbled off towards the chalets, Grace found herself alone with Paul.

'Are you glad you came back?' Paul asked.

Grace looked up. His kind face was lit with a smile, and for a moment she lost herself in him, forgetting everything, knowing only the moment that they stood together on the promenade while the world sauntered by around them.

She put her arms around his waist, and looked up at him. He looked a little nervous, but Grace pulled him forward and he took the hint, leaning down to give her a light kiss on the lips. The kiss lingered for a few seconds, then Paul drew away.

'You didn't answer my question.' He watched her with an expectant look on his face, one eyebrow raised, a corner of his mouth turned up in a small smile.

The wind had got up, bringing with it the first hint of the evening's chill. Around them, stalls were beginning to pack up, groups of tourists to head for the restaurants and the pubs. Above them, the sun still burned in a clear sky. Grace took a deep breath of fresh sea air and smiled, for the first time in forever feeling completely at peace.

'I just did,' she said.

ABOUT THE AUTHOR

CP Ward is a pen name of Chris Ward, the author of the dystopian *Tube Riders* series, the horror/science fiction *Tales of Crow* series, and the *Endinfinium* YA fantasy series, as well as numerous other well-received stand alone novels. In addition, he writes the critically acclaimed *Slim Hardy Mysteries* under the name of Jack Benton.

Summer at Blue Sands Cove is Chris's first summer book, after writing several Christmas books so far.

Expect more soon ...

Chris would love to hear from you:
www.amillionmilesfromanywhere.net
chrisward@amillionmilesfromanywhere.net

Printed in Dunstable, United Kingdom